A Clearer Fate

LEERY

authorHOUSE

AuthorHouse™
1663 Liberty Drive
Bloomington, IN 47403
www.authorhouse.com
Phone: 833-262-8899

© 2024 LEERY. All rights reserved.

No part of this book may be reproduced, stored in a retrieval system, or transmitted by any means without the written permission of the author.

Published by AuthorHouse 02/29/2024

ISBN: 979-8-8230-2226-2 (sc)
ISBN: 979-8-8230-2227-9 (hc)
ISBN: 979-8-8230-2228-6 (e)

Library of Congress Control Number: 2024903339

Print information available on the last page.

Any people depicted in stock imagery provided by Getty Images are models, and such images are being used for illustrative purposes only.
Certain stock imagery © Getty Images.

This book is printed on acid-free paper.

Because of the dynamic nature of the Internet, any web addresses or links contained in this book may have changed since publication and may no longer be valid. The views expressed in this work are solely those of the author and do not necessarily reflect the views of the publisher, and the publisher hereby disclaims any responsibility for them.

Contents

Chapter 1   Trip Down Memory Lane..................................1
Chapter 2   In the Midst of Things 6
Chapter 3   It Ain't Trickin' if You Got It..............................13
Chapter 4   Just Another Day 21
Chapter 5   Hard to Be Righteous When Life Can Stop
             for Pussy..26
Chapter 6   Shit Ain't the Same. Something Seems Strange....28
Chapter 7   Is Living and Dying a Lesson? 37
Chapter 8   A Broke Bastard with Potential............................43
Chapter 9   Veni, Vidi, Amavi (We Came, We Saw, We
             Loved)..55
Chapter 10   No New Niggas 61
Chapter 11   Meanwhile, Back in the Hood............................64
Chapter 12   Lord Knows 72
Chapter 13   It's the Unknown That Hits You the Hardest 75
Chapter 14   Ain't No Pussy like New Pussy 78
Chapter 15   Make Her Mind 81
Chapter 16   Grimy 86
Chapter 17   Jezebel..92
Chapter 18   In the Meantime, it's get Swole and get
             Clean Time 95
Chapter 19   Get the Fuck outta Dodge.................................97
Chapter 20   A clearer Fate..99

Malicious Wound (A Clearer Fate II)

Chapter 1   Ask God Why I'm Broke......................................103

I would like to take this opportunity to say thank you for purchasing *A Clearer Fate*. I hope you enjoy it. Thank you so much.
It is the client who turns small-time hustlers into giants.
Please use the link below to get a free live mixtape of Leery's songs that are quoted in *A Clearer Fate*.

https://m.soundcloud.com

Chapter 1

Trip Down Memory Lane

Let me take you back, in fact.
Long conversations in Starbucks.
Before the Starbucks, I played the waiting game.
I'm trying not to spit game.
I am trying to break the chain.
Is it a figment of my imagination,
Or I am loving these relations?
This goes out to you, as a matter of fact, my boo.
I painted a perfect picture of all the bullshit I put you through.
I knew the chemistry was there,
Mixed with a little bit of fear.

—Leery

I woke up this morning with a strange feeling that I couldn't identify. The aroma of the applewood smoked bacon cooking in the kitchen quickly turned that feeling into hunger. I hopped out of the sack and reached down to pick up my boxers before slowly strolling to the bathroom to drain the weasel. Then I brushed my chibs. I had to squeeze the tube of toothpaste hard just to fill up my toothbrush, but after that, everything was a go. Then I strolled slowly to the kitchen, overwhelmed by the aroma, which began taking over my body.

At the kitchen door, I first laid my eyes on Tracey's back, then glanced a little lower. Her pretty panties hugging her phat ass had me thinking, *What would I do without my baby?* I took a seat at the kitchen table to prepare for the feast: three pancakes, cheddar cheese eggs, four strips of applewood-smoked bacon, and a stupid-big cup of pineapple juice: the breakfast of champions. It was compliments of my better half, my one and only.

Tracey had gotten up early, knowing that I had to take my GED test today, went out of her way to make sure I had a full stomach so I could concentrate fully. I truly believed the saying "The way to a man's heart is through his stomach." Even though she already had my heart, the saying totally made sense. I recalled the day we first laid eyes on each other as if it were tattooed on my mind. No love-at-first-sight shit, but something inside me told me she should be mine. But I never knew she would make such an everlasting impact.

When I first approached Tracey, I felt the chemistry as if it had been orchestrated from above. We'd been together now for about seven years, more than enough time to settle down. As a Lil' Mo and Fabulous song came on the radio, Tracey damn near broke her neck just to turn the volume up. "Let's make it official. We ain't getting no younger, baby." Tracey sang along with an angelic voice.

"We're gonna be older way longer than we're gonna be younger."

"Damn, T, you ain't bullshitting. I feel you. "Like my nigger PAC said, 'I ain't mad at-cha.' Can I get my grub on? I feel like you are trying to son me like Mom and Dad and shit," I said. "This breakfast is banging."

"You know I get down in the kitchen."

"Especially breakfast. I put my foot in it."

"Damn, I hope not, Your crusty-ass toes."

"You see these three fingers, right?"

"What?"

"Read between the lines."

"I'm just fucking with you. But self-praise is no praise. You know the kitchen is the second-best place you showcase your skills, girl. Sit down and have breakfast with me, T."

"I have to get dressed. If I don't be out of the house at least a quarter till, I'll have to just squeeze into the packed train."

"Save your speech for the podium, Tracey."

"Good luck with your test, mister."

"Thanks."

"See you later, OK?"

"Yo, how are you gonna leave without giving me some sugar? Bring those melons over here. Fuck are you doing, yo?"

"Lock the door behind me."

Now alone with my thoughts, I was thinking about the Lil' Mo song and how Tracey might have had a valid point. Now Doctor Dré and Ed Lover were cracking jokes on the radio. My better half and I had come so far as a couple. Through all the circumstances we'd endured, our relationship was still authentic. Seven years ago, when I was a ghetto roundsman with the mindset that all money was legal, whether it came from a job, from the street, or from any little hustle like selling fiends little bags of Mama's Gold Medal flour out the kitchen, Tracey was able to keep my mind on positive things, instead of profitable schemes such as selling dreams. But it couldn't have been that bad if it stopped the hunger pains. It was all mathematics.

There I was posted on the strip, a roach clip burning my fingertips, with Black, Red, and Baby Blue. Red crushed the weed, and Black split the vanilla-flavored Dutch Master with his old-school orange box cutter before rolling an excellent blunt.

Black was a spur-of-the-moment-type dude who had thrown a battery in his own back, real as a motherfucker. Baby Blue was kind of the opposite, an actual laid-back quiet-storm type of individual trying to avoid confrontation. But when it was on, it was really on. My nigger Red, well, let's just say he was like a ticking bomb with a temper. Just imagine that. Me, P.P., a.k.a. Mr. Peep Plots, Paint Pictures, and Purchase Pussy, was just a laid-back, cool, calm, and collected type of dude who picked up everything, a real observant thinker.

Since we all seemed to be smokaholics, Red's statement "Puff, puff, pass" seemed more like a recording than a request.

"I'm trying to get my lungs dirty like everybody else," Red uttered.

As I passed the little bastard that kept us blasted to Red, Cashout threw Black a package of Backwoods to roll up his bright green jar of hydro that he'd just pulled out from his Champion hooded sweater pocket. Cashout was the type to con his way into your wife's satin lace panties. He was born with the gift of gab. I don't think I'd ever seen him without a dime or better. He had that pimp juice. Tracey had once been in his stable before she got laid off and chose another. How ironic is that? I knew I couldn't turn no ho into a housewife, simple and plain. But people and times tended change. We lived and learned to put our pride aside and use our past as a ghetto guide.

> A candy girl with no poison in her veins,
> Turning tricks. Ain't no shame in her game.
> Double the amount, you can even run a train.
> Word through the grapevine, she has some excellent brain.
> All mind now. What a shame.
> You know God works in mysterious ways.

*Can't knock nobody's hustle to get chips like Lay's.
With a little unconditional love, you'll be amazed.*
—Leery

    Malaysia was considered Tracey's right lung. They'd been childhood peers, and their relationship had lasted through the years. They'd gone to the same public junior high school and high school, and now they were distant strangers to me. Monica, Tina, and Malaysia were like the Three Amigos. Rarely would you see one without the other. Malaysia was a care bear with much love in her heart, real shit, no perjury. She could hold a nigger down and also throw it down in the kitchen, always willing to feed a nigger—one of those culinary art graduates who loved their craft. Tina, let's call her a pimpstress. She stood about five feet six inches in height, was thick and curvy, and was half black and half Chinese—a superbad bitch. Nobody could tell her that she did not have a gold mine between her legs. She had a skill, or a gift, for milking ballers who were wide awake but still asleep.
    Then there was the ebony queen Monica, stripper by night and law school student by day. She had a Coca-Cola bottle shape and a model's face with long hair down to her ass crack—sweet as the brown sugar in candied yams. Last but not least was Lucy. With a coffee complexion, she was slim and tall with a mean kickstand that made her onion look rounder than a basketball. Bless ya, mama.

Chapter 2

In the Midst of Things

Learn how to think ahead.
So I fight with my pen.
Death to all the frenemies.
Actors need Oscars 'cause they pretend.
A few facts in life:
With the good comes the bad.
That's the facts of life.

—Leery

Tracey had grown up in the murder capital of New York, Bushwick in Brooklyn, in a single-family home where her mother played the role of father. Tracey had been a vibrant precocious little girl, full of potential. Talk about a future master of her environment. Mother and daughter were a best-friends team, a bond that was never to be tampered with. Tracey had never really had a relationship with her father because Yaritza had conceived at an early age, so early that it didn't even matter who the father was. It was too early to notice her pregnancy but too late to extract the growing human being inside her body. Tracey as a little girl had been overdeveloped. She advanced in the school system. That made her mother very proud. But as Tracey grew up, her pact with her mother started to fade. Yaritza became more concerned with the fast life and the players.

A Clearer Fate

Yaritza was a stunning woman. She had no problem attracting the opposite sex. Her curvy figure put some of the younger women to shame. On one typical night at the Baby Grand, a plus-size strip club in Bed-Stuy, Brooklyn, the sexy Yaritza, working as a bartender, intrigued a well-known street boss, Frog, who was respected and feared. Her beauty was no match for the dancers, and her ass in those jeans caused men to crave her undivided attention.

"Let me get an orange juice and a bottle of water," Frog said.

"You must be new. I've never seen you around here," Yaritza said, speaking loud to be heard over the music.

"I am going to be a regular if they keep you serving the drinks. You're so beautiful," Frog replied.

"Thank you." Yaritza blushed, handing him his orange juice and bottle of water.

Soon, Frog introduced her to the powder-your-nose world. Nose candy became Yaritza's everything.

Now that Yaritza was a certified candy girl, Frog used her and abused her, then made his move. Porkin Bean Jeremy—PBJ for short—was able to detect a weakness and was also able to sew it up. A smooth-talking gentleman, Porkin Bean Jeremy fed Yaritza's nose religiously just for the opportunity to caress her perfect figure.

One night at her apartment, earlier than usual, Porkin Bean spotted Tracey going to relieve her bladder of red Kool-Aid. She was wearing an oversized T-shirt and some panties that accentuated her young but overdeveloped curves. Porkin Bean had to be the first to taste that. Yaritza was 100 percent against it, wanting to shield her daughter from Porkin Bean's lustful gaze.

"She is just a baby. She's too young," Yaritza spoke with a gut full of passion. Thinking back to her own strange early encounters, Yaritza wanted better for her child.

Porkin Bean Jeremy confessed with an evil smirk, "I have something even better than your usual pick-me-up."

"What do you mean?" Yaritza snatched the substance out of his hand like a hard candy abuser. She inhaled the brownish powder: heroin. It had a different effect on her body than did the white substance she was accustomed to.

"Just relax. It will take you where you need to be."

Porkin Bean noticed the nod all too well. He checked to see if Yaritza was breathing before making his way to Tracey's room. Tracey's mom was gone on the new product. She couldn't even hear her own flesh and blood crying for help. Jeremy got there just in time, before Tracey could say a word. He manhandled her and threw her on her bed.

"Get off me!" Tracey tried to fight and scream, her tears beginning to fall. She had no say in the matter. Porkin Bean Jeremy parted her legs using her feet. Before she could kick him in the face, he drove his face between her legs. She continued to try to fight him off. Soon her kicking and screaming turned into a feeling of indifference. Not sure how to feel, she stopped resisting. Soon, pleasure was written all over her face. She began to thrust back and forth. At that second, she lost control of her own body. She smothered Porkin Bean's face with her natural juices. Porkin Bean continued his tongue assault until her body collapsed.

Tracey lay there in a half-awake state, halfway happy it was over, not expecting his fat ass to climb on top of her. She was too weak and soaked to stop Porkin Bean from placing a condom on and placing his little wiener inside her. A puddle of sweat began to form on her chest. PBJ grinds into her as delicately as he could. A few minutes after that, he slid his penis out of her, took the condom off, and squirted his babies all over her face. Tracey flinched from the hotness of his liquid.

Porkin Bean laughed as he pulled his pants up. He threw two fifty-dollar bills and two hundred-dollar bills on the dresser and left the tiny one-bedroom apartment. Tracey heard the door slam and decided to get up to take a hot shower. She noticed her mom looking as if she were taking a peaceful nap with her back against the back of the sofa. Tracey continued to her destination. After the hot water was gone, she stepped out of the shower and marched back to her room. Yaritza was in the same spot as she'd been when Tracey went into the shower thirty-three minutes ago. Tracey noticed the greenbacks on top of the dresser. Knowing that her mother would claim it, she decided to take two of the bills.

Tracey's mom finally popped out of her trance before Tracey closed her eyes and forgot such a cruel act occurred. Yaritza hadn't a care in the world once she learned about what had happened. No worried statement, no compassionate hug, just focusing on the green. Tracey no longer felt she loved her mother. Yaritza sat next to Tracey and just stared a hole in her face. Tracey kept her own eyes on the floor as tears ran down her face. Yaritza was too occupied with the urge to satisfy her craving to console her daughter.

"You are ready now," Yaritza said, handing Tracey her fifty dollars and keeping the remaining hundred for herself. Tracey's mind wandered, thinking about giving her mother the money she had put away. But then she dismissed the idea. She gave her mother a hug and went to sleep.

Yaritza hit the bully in search of her newfound friend. She was open like a window now with a new addiction.

*

Boredom was typical in the summertime in Brooklyn, New York. This evening was no different. After a long day of working hard, or hardly working, Tracey, Malaysia, and Tina finally received their first summer youth checks, which seemed to be burning a hole in their pockets. The sun disappeared. It was officially dark outside, but early as hell.

"This Friday night has to be different," Tracey told the pack.

"Let's go to the movies," Tina suggested.

"To see what?" Malaysia spit out quickly.

"I don't know. We can go chill in Gowanus with Lucy."

"Let me stop you right there. Lucy is always involved in some drama with them bitches over them niggers. I ain't trying to be around them fake-ass baby ballers tonight. Let's go to the rink."

"That shit is a good idea, even though it's full of a bunch of F.A.Gs., those fake-ass gangsters. Let's roll."

The Empire skating rink was the perfect place to unwind. The prestigious area was a staple of the girls' with a lot of familiar faces and many of their favorite songs. The wait in line was quick.

"At least they got metal detectors," Malaysia said a little too loud, catching the eye of a security guard, who smiled and winked at her.

"Damn this long-ass line," Tracey said. "We still gotta get our skates." Tracey glanced to her left and spotted Arthur. She felt butterflies in her stomach and blushed every time she saw Arthur, but she'd never told him how she felt. Malaysia, knowing her bestie well, knew Tracey had a super crush. After all the different girls she had seen with Arthur, Malaysia had come to the conclusion that he was wrong for her friend.

"Tracey, that nigger is a slut," Malaysia said, scolding her friend because she was eating up his thirsty stares.

"Maybe he ain't found the right one."

"You think you can change the game?"

"I know I can."

"Shoot your shot, diva."

Rolling around like a pro, attempting to show off, Arthur fell hard on his ass bone, causing people to stare. Tracey, determined to win him over, skated over to ensure he hadn't broken any bones. "Are you good?" she asked, with one hand over her mouth so he couldn't see her laughing at his clumsy ass.

"Yeah. I think I bruised four bones in my gluteus maximus," Arthur said, massaging his butt cheek.

"If you did that, you would still be on the floor crying like a bitch," Tracey added.

"You are a care bear."

"What?"

"Why did you come over here?"

"I can leave."

"Why would you want to do a thing like that? I need a hug to feel better. Damn, you smell good. What perfume is that?"

"It's called 'nunya.'"

"What?"

"None of your business."

"I walked right into that one."

"Right."

"Who are you here with?"

"My girls."

"Where is your little girlfriend Tenisha?"

"That's my people. We are cool, but we're not together right now."

"You are my new sugar pie, honeybunch."

"Is that right?"

"I was getting ready to skate over there and hit you with the old-school letter: 'Do you wanna go steady? Yes, no, or maybe?'"

"You're crazy. What high school did you get accepted to, Arthur?"

"Aviation and Thomas Edison. I'm fucking with Thomas Edison."

"That's all the way in Queens."

"The G train to the F train, then I'm straight."

"True that, if you don't mind getting up early every day."

"Tracey, I know you got accepted to all of them, right? With your Einstein ass."

"What? Shut up. For your information, I only picked Maxwell, Thomas Jefferson, and Sarah J."

"I bet you got into all of them."

"Yes I did, but I'm going to Sarah J. because it's close to home. And my girls got accepted too."

"Damn, ya going to the same college too?"

"Maybe."

"Are y'all going to marry the same dude too? Don't make plans without me, because you are still going to be mine."

"Arthur, I'm not yours now."

"Yes you are. You mustn't have gotten the memo. I am firing my secretary. Let's skate together to ensure I don't fall and break my butt bones." Tracey laughed while holding Arthur's hand, pulling him back to the skating rink floor.

Chapter 3

It Ain't Trickin' if You Got It

> Meanwhile, back in the hood, where it's all good,
> With the nine on me like I wish a nigger would.
> Small section of casual fiend queens
> I accumulate. Thank God for the fiends.
> Jealousy and envy: that's why I wear this Glock
> in my jeans.
> Stash the heat before I daydream.
>
> —Leery

Daydreams was the name of a local strip club that I frequented.

"I'm addicted to this place," I said to Black. He ignored my statement. "What are you drinking, P.P.? First round on me."

"Hennessy and cranberry, my dude."

Black retrieved the yak. Out of nowhere, this phat-ass red bone started grinding her huge butt cheeks against my body to the tune of an ancient Jamaican song. "'I need some action, tender satisfaction,'" I sang along while my eyes focused on shorty's booty cleavage, not paying attention to Black, who was holding my drink in my face with a big Kool-Aid smile on his. Black screamed, "One!" and began moving toward the rear of the club. As he was walking off, Phat Ass had my full attention in more than one way. She introduced her bubble as Mariann.

"P.P.," I replied as I palmed her booty like I ain't want to let it go. As I stared her down, I realized she was easy on the eyes.

"Do you want a lap dance?" Mariann asked as sexily as possible.

"Not right now. Maybe later." I'd holler at her. My having declined her offer caused her disappointment, which I could see written all over her face, but who the hell cared? Doing my rounds, I peeped Black in the zone with this dark-skinned bubble, so I let him be. I drank down the rest of what was in my cup and went up to the bar for another drink. My song began to erupt in the club.

"'I need a gangster bitch. I want a gangster bitch, yo. I need a, I want a, I need a gangster bitch who don't sleep and who don't play sticking up niggers from around the fucking way.'" I swear, that Apache song was the joint for every hood nigger who lived a precise lifestyle. As I sang along for the second time that night, Black hit the bar right on time to replenish his drink. After the brown water embraced my body, Black turned right. I turned left.

Halfway through my second cup, I was posted on the wall enjoying the stage show: two land mine freaks getting it on. Candy and Alexus had me ready to hit the stage and slide right in from the way they were licking each other's ass cracks. That was when I got a heavy feeling letting me know it was time to release some brown water.

In the restroom, I overheard the conversation of two young bandanna cats, the one telling his homey the importance of eating before putting that yak in his system. The mess on the toilet seat and the floor should have been a reminder. I washed my hands, picked up my drink, and kept moving. Black was on his way to follow in the footsteps I had taken just a few minutes ago. I could tell by the way he walked fast to get inside. The yak will do it to you every time. Once he was finished, he gave a nod and went back to the dance floor.

As I was bopping my head to the Naughty by Nature joint "O.P.P.," I saw this chocolate-colored broad with a neon outfit that brought out her complexion. She had a sexy ass.

"Do you want to do a lap dance?" she asked.

My mind said no, but my body said yes. The DJ started to switch back to the reggae tunes, and a Mad Cobra song blessed our ears.

"This is a sexy song," Neon Booty said, giving me a look that said, *You can have whatever you'd like.* She worked her hips in an aerobics-like rhythm as if we were fucking in 3D. It must have been the Hennessy I was sipping because I felt that we were doing the damn thing without doing the damn thing. Neon Booty's seduction skills were A+. The bitch had the audacity to ask if I liked it. I never replied, but I was sure she took that as a yes. Lord knows I was ready to part her thighs like that dude Moses who parted the Red Sea.

The DJ announced the last call for alcohol, which made me check the time. I saw no sign of Black from where I was sitting. I was sure my son would not kick rocks without me. Phat Ass from earlier walked past and smiled like she knew her phat ass fit the description at the moment. After the third song went off, sexy Neon Booty got her ass up. I dipped into my stash to give her a well-earned tip for her seductive service, then I caught up with Black. His slurred speech told me he was bent but still sipping. Figuring that my son was ready to skate and go home to wifey, I ensured that he got into a cab before I returned to take a leak and find Phat Ass to give her my math.

Still sipping, I was now so hungry that my breath stank. Ready to make a move, I said fuck it and asked Phat Ass, a.k.a. Mariann, if she wanted to roll to get something to eat. Her smile answered my question. She told me to meet her in the parking lot in five minutes. Ten minutes later, to my surprise, she came out with Neon Booty. I was posted on the lean on my hooptie, rollin' some dookie.

On my way down Hillside Avenue to 169th Street to the International House of Pancakes, Neon Booty said, "Can I get my lungs dirty, P.P.?" Mariann considered her girlfriend's statement.

"H-e-double-hockey-sticks no. Get your own. Can't touch a dime of mine." That was my reply, but I passed the joint anyway. Mariann passed it to Neon Booty. I found out later that Neon Booty's name was Sasha.

As I parked the hooptie, I realized how phat Sasha's ass was without the strobe light on it. In her regular jeans, her booty appeared to need some oxygen.

I picked a corner booth in the cut, but the women wanted to sit on each side of me for some reason. I wasn't complaining.

The waiter dropped off a few menus and a few glasses of ice-cold H_2O, which looked tasty like a motherfucker. Ninety seconds later, he asked if we were ready to order.

"Yes, a short stack with a hash brown platter and a large pineapple juice." I told myself, *Fuck that "ladies first" shit. We all get our food at the same time anyhow.*

Mariann ordered a cheese omelet, beef sausage, grits, and home fries with peppermint tea.

"I don't know what I want," Sasha said. "Let me get the same thing as him, but with orange juice."

As the girls started to count their singles, I decided to go take a leak and wash up.

"Yo, I'll be right back," I said, grabbing my phone to make sure Black made it home safely. I walked away and dialed.

After five rings, a sweet female voice answered, saying, "Hello?"

"Can I speak to Black?" I asked Tiffany, his wife.

"He is in the shower."

I told her to tell him to holler at me in a few, saying it was nothing important. I checked my missed calls. There was one from Red. I decided I'd holler at him at a more reasonable hour. Back at the table, the food was just arriving, piping hot. The women went to wash up and do whatever it was they did. I said my grace and stuffed my face. The women returned and let the food meet the liquor in their systems. A loud conversation at another table snapped me out of the daze I was in, imagining both broads going down on me like a basement. I guess patience is a virtue. Full as hell, I was ready to spark an L and do whatever.

"What are you thinking about, P.P.?" Sasha asked.

"How both your lips would feel." But what came out was what was popping. Sasha must have been a mind reader because suddenly she slid under the table and started rubbing my tool.

"You're gonna wake the dead." Her deep throat caused a change in my laid-back demeanor, which I'm sure was highly noticeable in my facial expression. She made me release in less than four minutes. Then she put me back in my boxers and blew me a kiss that made me happy like a fat person at an all-you-can-eat buffet.

I paid the waiter and included a hefty tip, genuinely anxious to get to the hotel, motel, Holiday Inn. It was about a fifteen-minute drive to the Comfort Inn on 136th Street and Rockaway Boulevard. The ride was silent except for Hot 97, which was thumbing the latest urban song by Ja Rule, "Holla Holla." I started thinking about how I wanted to stretch the insides of both these twats, word to everything I loved. I finally reached my destination. With no hesitation, I parked the whip in the parking lot.

"Y'all want anything from the twenty-four-hour joint?" I asked.

"Bring me some Funyuns and some Lemonheads," Sasha requested.

"I just want a Fanta," Mariann replied.

I needed some essentials: some roll-ups, some T-shirts, Red Bull, water, and two Snickers. After I'd come back from the store and was back in the parking lot, the women looked either ready to go or ready to get it crackin'. I felt kind of strange for some reason, but I ignored it.

> Hotel clerk greeting. I'm fiending. Give the nod to my young niggas who a bleeding. Short overnight stay. Can't shake the feeling these bum bitches scheming. Fifth floor. Make a left down the hall, hoping they'll swallow my offspring and all. Decent four walls. First thing, take a leak. Sit on the bed with my back against the wall. Spark my roach clip from the car trip black like my lungs who need finger tips
>
> —Leery

"I'll be back. I gotta get some ice." Mariann stepped out of the room with the ice bucket. Sasha stripped down to her birthday suit and hopped into the shower. After less than one minute had passed, she was back in the room with a conniving look. Maybe the chronic had me overanalyzing as usual.

"Why the fuck didn't you go to a hotel with a Jacuzzi?" Mariann asked, her hands on her hips.

"I don't know."

Since Neon Booty was in the shower, I decided to help her clean her private parts. I lathered her onion up. Mariann decided to join the party. The size of Mariann's booty kind of demanded attention. Just brushing up against her had me ready to make her bend over and lean. But my raincoats were on the bed.

Sasha washed the rest of the soap off her body and stepped out of the bathroom. While I took a shower, Phat Ass sat on the edge of the tub, massaging my third leg before slowly kissing the tip, then spitting on the tip as if cursing it. She had me making love to her mouth. Then she just stopped and walked out, leaving me feeling like I was going to explode.

The girls were already exploring each other in their birthday suits when I walked out of the bathroom. I found it hard to wipe the Kool-Aid smile off my grille. I sparked my L again and just watched, enjoying the show. I cracked open my Red Bull and took three to four gulps. When the show stopped, both women approached me and threw me on the bed. Mariann went to work from the slit in my boxers, filling her jaws. Sasha sat on my face. I had no choice but to go fishing with my tongue. Her pearl oyster tasted like banana cake.

I was a fan of banana cake. Mariann was nice on the microphone. I screamed, "Knowledge is power!" as her saliva dripped down my thigh. Sasha moaned heavily. I had to spread her butt cheeks just to be able to breathe through my nose. Mariann ripped off my boxers and tongue-kissed my third-leg soldier. As she continued to cover my top like a shirt, Sasha switched places with Phat Ass. Then, Sasha, deep-throating me, sent me over the edge. No longer able to hold it back, I released straight down her throat.

Having gotten my focus back thanks to the girls, I strapped up for the pussy war that awaited me. Phat Ass hopped on the wood backward. Sasha stood up, but I pulled her down, face-to-back with Phat Ass. I plucked her areolas and massaged her third nipple, then I dipped the tip of my tongue into her asshole. That must have caused lightning to shoot through her body. She started grabbing my head like a dude getting some good sloppy-toppy. I took a mental picture before seeing Mariann's ass in the doggy-style position. I slowed down my thrusts. Sasha took a recess. I was digging Mariann's guts, trying my hardest not to nut. Her ass looked beautiful on all fours. Then Phat Ass suggested, more like demanded, that I throw it in her stanker. I spit in her ass cavity and eased in with perfection.

While I was long-stroking Phat Ass, Sasha got back into the game and started massaging my nuts. I could not reset or restart—whatever you call it. She slid off the tee like a good bitch and swallowed my babies like a pro. Sasha put a fresh tee on with her lips.

"Love that extra shit," I said. Sasha assumed the position. I pulled her to the edge of the bed, put one leg up, and pounded that shit like I was possessed. I put my finger in her ass crack before I decided to slide right in.

"You're gonna love my vise grip," Sasha told me, "the way it wiggles with every stroke."

Even though I had to pay, I told myself, *It ain't trickin' if you got it.*

Chapter 4

Just Another Day

> It's just another day, drowning my troubles with a deuce-deuce.
> These bitches is loose.
> Most of these niggas sweet like juice.
> Sidetrack who? Family matters like the Winslows.
> I guess the love disappears like the wind blows.
> —Leery

"How many books do you have?" Tracey asked Lucy, her partner, as they were playing spades. She was down by eighty points.

"Six, maybe seven."

"Cool."

Monica suggested to Tina that they go aboard. "I know that's right." I didn't have any books. "Your phone is vibrating, Tina."

"Cut the music down."

"Hello? ... Yes. How the fuck did you forget where my building is, Leery? It must be all that contraband you are smoking. ... I will meet you at the Chinese restaurant. When you leave the train station, it is right on the left side of the street. What kind of liquor did you bring? ... What do you mean, what kind do I drink? Now you're going to answer a question with a question. I don't know. We'll decide when you get here. ... OK, call me when you touch down." Tina delayed the game further with her cell phone glued to her ear, like if she missed one word, it would be a matter of life and death. After two minutes, she returned to the game with a Kool-Aid smile, singing her theme song: "All the honeys getting money, playing niggas like dummies, milking another baller tonight." The women, all too familiar with the scheme, laughed among themselves. "Girl, this nigga is beyond fine," Tina aid with admiration. "After Paul dropped me off yesterday, his whip slowed down at an intersection."

"What's his name?" Tracey asked.

"Nitro."

"Where is he from?"

"Nosy."

"Inquiring minds want to know," Tracey added.

"He is from Minnesota. He's here visiting some of his people. That navigator, he pushed the diamonds on his neck. He just reeks of cheese."

"She got an eye-hustling appraisal on his frozen water," Tracey replied with laughter.

"Be careful, girl," Monica said with concern in her voice. "Them hustling niggas ain't shit. What makes you think he is a dope boy? He could be a businessman."

"I don't know, but like I said, I'm draining another baller tonight."

*

"Yo, my dude, pay attention. I ain't got time for fuckups and bullpen therapy," Stupid Face warned his thirsty Young Gunner as they moved in on their prey, whom Stupid assumed were sleeping. Stupid had gotten word through the grapevine that niggas were making a pretty penny, a small fortune really, from the new spot smack-dab in the middle of the hood. He didn't take kindly to out-of-towners coming up without him eating. A plot was in the making, and his thirsty Young Gunner was relating. After hours of playing police, and after having staked out the joint for days, looking for the perfect time to strike like a cobra, Stupid, making sure the correct number of team members had kicked rocks before making his move, concluded that he had just witnessed eight out of nine members vanish in their two vehicles. He figured that the odds would be uneven. Easy money; easy to rob them and say thank you. He told himself, *Now that's keeping it gangster.* But to his surprise, two members hadn't left the premises.

In broad daylight, Stupid Face ducked behind a familiar fiend to make his entrance. Young Gunner went around back to hold him down. Stupid Face knocked the young cat out cold with his gun, and the fiend hauled ass down the block until he was out of sight. Then Stupid Face proceeded to open the back door for Young Gunner to accompany him in the search. Gunner took the top. Stupid took what remained. He came across a few dusty-rubber-band stacks of twenties and tens. His eyes lit up when he saw six Ziploc bags full of light green weed.

On his way to the exit, Stupid found the barrel a Glock 19 pointed in his face. Before he could utter a word, his brain was splattered all over the shooter's shoes and the wall. His body dropped instantly. With no idea of what had just transpired, Gunner approached the area, having heard the noise, and suffered the same fate. The first shot sent him to the bottom of the stairs, where his body was greeted with the remaining bullets left in the clip.

Maybe greed is a disease.

*

Red and Blue were posted up a few blocks from the p's, patiently waiting in a Chinese restaurant for Asia to carry her ass. The pretty Chinese waitress took my order, speaking in a lovely accent as if she were fresh off the plane from China. Her ass was surprisingly phat. At first, I thought I was bugging out. Probably the chronic had me seeing shit, hallucinating and shit. But when my man Blue cosigned that shit, I knew I wasn't bugging.

"This Chinese chick got a phat ass," I said.

"Are you trying to glaze her buns?"

"That's rare, like subtriplets out this motherfucker." I mimicked her accent, which caused her to smile. I had been about to drop my mack dosage shit when Asia walked in. Being the player that I am, I managed to scribble my number on the menu before I broke out. The expression on her face let me know she was hip to the bullshit. I grabbed my wings and fries and made my exit.

"After I told you I was cooking, I know you didn't buy anything to eat," Asia said like a ghetto chick, moving her hands.

"Relax. This shit right here is a snack, Asia. You sound like an annoying wife. Shut up. And tell me where the liquor spot is at, Ms. Nag."

Back on the block, Black and Leery were burning a filthy lung-brain stimulator and freestyling. Leery was sick with the flow.

> Rocking Tims with trees. Smoking trees.
> Never run in a bird bitch without a tee.
> In the hood, you lucky if you find l-o-v-e.
> Much respect to my bees and my cees.
> I'm not even Latin, but I'm a king.
> They call me the Piano Man. I be moving keys

Like four hundred plus six hundred. All my niggas is g's.
I could be dead broke but rich in the hood with loyalty.
Information the new currency.

—Leery

Cashout stepped onto the stoop with this bitch who looked as if he'd pulled her off a picture in a magazine, pretty ass, all outdoors. I just wanted to fuck her face and every other penetrable area all at once.

Cashout stated, "Pass the little bastard that keeps me blasted."

"Who shorty?" Blue asked.

"This is the daughter of my new connect, Marisol. I'm back on my feet. Only time will tell. You are going to see my pocket swell, and I tell no tales."

In sequence, Cashout passed Red a uniquely flavored Dutch Master—cognac—with instructions to roll up a decent-size cigar.

"That's what I'm talking about," Red stated. "*Pásame ese fuego,* ma."

Marisol shortly produced a twenty bag of some sticky green that probably would have us stuck contemplating the truth.

Chapter 5

Hard to Be Righteous When Life Can Stop for Pussy

Shorty was like, "What you need? I got you."
I'm like, "Who you want to bleed?"
I pop Duke. I stop Duke. He a memory.
History fucking with a felony.
I'm just fronting like Pharrell, dodging jail.
Broken scale. I can't measure it out.

—Leery

Jason reclined in his seat. Sasha sucked him to attention before she hopped aboard. As he fondled her butt cheeks, she nibbled on his ear. As she slowly moving up and down on his lap, her moans could be heard outside the vehicle if one was walking past and listening closely.
"I love you," Jason stated, as he released his offspring into Sasha's tunnel of love.
"I love you too," Sasha repeated the statement. The lovebirds cuddled for a while. Then Sasha straightened her thong and pulled her skirt down. As soon as she put her ass back in the passenger's seat, a loud noise shattered the driver's-side windows. Jason's brain matter splattered all over her face. Too scared to scream and too stunned to move, she just sat there trembling

for the next fifteen minutes, before the police snapped her out of the trance she was in. Even after Sasha returned to reality, she still could not help the cops. Her statement was that all she'd seen was her man's brains all over her face. That was the reason she became traumatized. Everything after the sex was a blank. With no other witnesses and a traumatized victim, Officer Bigbits and his partner, Polluten, had their hands full. As they proceeded with the investigation, their superiors would demand some answers.

Chapter 6

Shit Ain't the Same. Something Seems Strange

I was blind to the facts,
A little slower to react.
These haters smell victory,
Assuming I am history.
Realistically out of sight, never out of mind.
Pringles and Lay's.
That's why I'm on my grind.

—Leery

"Yo, what's good?"

"Who is this?"

"This P.P., nigger."

"Oh, yo, I called you last night. Why didn't you pick up the phone?"

"Homey, you sound like one of these bitches. For real."

"I'm five minutes away."

"No doubt."

"Bring some roll-ups."

"I got you." The sound of the phone vibrating on the dresser caused Black to grab his phone. "Who is this?"

"Yo, come open the door."

"What's good, my nigga? What it is?"

"It ain't shit, word. After your drunk ass went home, son, I played the club for a while longer. I could not skate before I had to drop my math to this breezy with an extraterrestrial phat ass. I had to call her Phat Ass because I forgot the bitch's name. Check this shit out: fucked around, wind up at IHOP, then went to the hotel, motel, Holiday Inn. No need for me to stress the rest. You see your band from these episodes, family man. But the bonus was the chocolate piece who stole the show. I think I love them bitches, all jokes aside." Laughter escaped Black's mouth. He almost choked on smoke at the same time.

"Mr. Trick-or-Treat, and it ain't even Halloween. I know them hos. They could have lined that ass up."

"Son, how you sound? It's me, P.P., Peep Plots, Paint Pictures, Purchase Pussy. I do what I do. But on some serious shit, Stupid got popped yesterday evening."

"Say word. How do you know, nigger?"

"Deborah called me like fifteen minutes ago crying and shit."

"That bitch he laid up with in the B-cross?"

"Yeah, son. She had something to do with it?"

"I don't know, but I doubt it."

"Where did that shit go down?"

"In the hood, across on Merrick, close to that public school."

"Ain't that where the new spot is?"

"Exactly, my dude."

"So, it had to be them out-of-town niggers, or some other shit jumped off. I'll holler at this fiend. Maybe crackhead Clifford can shed some light."

"Damn, he is always thirsty and shit. Don't know how to be easy and shit. Love my nigger, though. I'm gonna miss my nigger."

"Let's go get some more brain scrambler."

"Let me slip my shit on. Something just doesn't seem right. Would he try to ride on them niggers?"

"Not for Dolo, I'm sure. He would have called me most likely. Shit is crazy."

"I'm clueless, P.P. After we blaze another L, maybe we can get a higher learning. Feel me?"

"My shit on E. Gotta get some gas."

"Do you, my dude?"

"How is the new edition?"

"Everything is good. It is a must to adapt to family life. I had to retire my player jersey and all that shit, na mean? That street shit got a time limit. That's why I am on some chuck chill-out shit."

"I can dig that."

"Yo, son, you think I should holler at Deborah?"

"For what?"

"She might need her pipes unclogged."

"P.P., you an extra grimy-ass nigger. Son ain't even buried, and already you wanna pull her satin panties off."

"How do you know they are satin?"

"What?"

"I'm just saying. That ass is phat."

"Stop at the liquor store so I can pour out a little liquor."

"What the fuck is the deal with Blue and Red?"

"Those niggers probably got their mouths open and shit somewhere. You know it is getting ready to be on."

"I'm just trying to chill."

"Try to call them niggers and see what they up to."

"Yo, what is it? This Black. Holler when you get this message." Turning to P.P., he said, "Blue ain't picked up. Let me try Red. Shit.

"Yo, my nigger, what's cracking? Where are you at?"
"I'm with Blue. We are in the boonies over in Pomonok."
"Blue next to you? Tell son to hit me later."
"No doubt. They got their faces in some ass in Pomonok."
"Nigger, don't try to put ass-eating on them."
"You are the only one who does that shit."
"I shouldn't even blaze behind your nasty ass."
"More chronic for me, nigger."
"I put money on it that you ate both of them strippers' butts."
"No I didn't. What do I look like, a nasty ass-eater?"
"If I ask them, what're they gonna say?"
"They're gonna say, 'P.P. don't get down like that.'"
"Yeah, right, they fuck around and say, 'He nasty as he wanna be. Just the way I like him.'"
"All day I dream about sex."
"Keep it real, you ate their booties like groceries, Purchased Pussy."
"I don't know what you are talking about."

*

Stepping out of the manager's office with something to contemplate, Malaysia didn't want, or better yet think she could handle, the new responsibility. As head chef at the prestigious Michael Jordan's Steak House, she had the option to relocate to another franchise if she decided to.

Malaysia was fine with her sous chef position. The money was excellent, and the hours were great. The bonus was that the staff members were friendly and easy to get along with. As the saying goes, the job at a different location was hers if she wanted it. Stuck in her head because of the manager's offer, she had to think really hard. Yes, she would earn more money, but her whole life would change. Dedication is the backbone of any culinary mastermind.

Dialing her bestie to get her opinion and help with making her decision, Malaysia had a few months to get back to the manager, Mr. Logan, with her answer. Her call went straight to voice mail. Deciding to call her girl back at a later time, she grabbed her headphones to prepare for the long train ride. While making her way to the iron horse to head home, she was startled by a gentle tap on her shoulder and turned swiftly to look behind her. She was genuinely surprised to see Arthur, the short-order cook who was always staring in her face with a Kool-Aid smile.

"Miss me?" Arthur asked. "It's Friday. Let's have a drink." He spoke in a smooth Barry White voice that moistened her triangle.

"Why the hell not? First round on you, Artie."

"I like how you said that. It is Arturo in Spanish."

"Do you speak Spanish?"

"Yes, but only the nasty words."

"Why did I even ask you? What's a good place besides here?"

"My place. You gotta be a bit more specific, girl."

"I meant a public place."

"I know, I'm just fucking with you. Get your panties out of a bunch. Damn. Relax. So, you're going to be the head vagina in charge?"

"Still deciding."

"I feel that. More money ain't everything. Sometimes less is more."

"Shit, when your arms are short and you have deep pockets, it's everything."

"Loosen up, girl. I wonder why the executive chef resigned."

"Better offer, most likely. Pretty young dude."

"Who the hell cares? I got the 'I don't give a fuck' in me, and it's stuck in me."

"True indeed. I might take the position. But—"

"But nothing, Malaysia. If you want it, take it. If you don't, fuck it."

"That's easier said than done. They are expecting me."

"Enough with that work shit. We are off the clock. Let's enjoy this time. I rarely get one-on-one time with you unless you are barking in a special order or some shit."

"I'm not that bad."

"Outside looking in. I'm joking. Everybody must play their part. We are a team, na mean? Now tell me about your scars. Did your mama beat ya?"

"Shut up, Arthur."

"Seriously, Malaysia, I want to get to know you outside the kitchen."

"OK, what do you want to know?"

"Your bra size, your panty colors, or any big draws. Are your sock colors fading? For real, what do you like to do besides throw down in the kitchen?

"I wish I had my bong right now. You smoke, Arthur, Mister Goody Two-shoes?"

"No."

"I figured you didn't."

"I used to get my lungs dirty religiously."

"Why did you quit?"

"It ain't the life for me. I guess I grew out of that shit. I had a ten-dollar-a-day habit, seventy dollars a week, two hundred eighty dollars a month. That's three thousand three hundred sixty dollars a year. That's not even counting the roll-up. True story."

"Damn, you were a weed head."

LEERY

"I prefer to call it 'escaping reality often.' It all started with one, maybe two pulls. I was high out of my mind, extra bent, overwhelmed by the spell. The blunt had me."

"Let me find out you were a fiend."

"I guess that was the hors d'oeuvre and shit. A dime bag every day was the main course. I started chipping in with my homeys for two or maybe three dollars a day. Soon enough, I was smoking a nickel bag of weed dolo daily."

"What does dolo mean?"

"It means solo, alone, by my lonesome."

"My bad."

"Still on my escalating smokaholic bullshit, I graduated to a dime bag every day. They call me Cee Fell. I puff L's until my brain swells. And I tell no tales."

"Why do they call you Cee Fell?"

"You are a listening junkie. That was my rap name."

"You got a little flow? Let me hear something."

"OK, I got you: Can love truly rewrite the past? / Can thugs unite to get this cash? / Does weed mix perfectly with hash? / How 'bout grilled salmon, asparagus, and some garlic mashed? / Red wine, Cîroc as a matter of fact. Some Henny. / American Jamaican. Matter of fact, she Trini. / My third leg down her throat. Her hand on my hip bone just like my semi. / Nine outta ten niggas-in-the-hood guineas / taught her how to say 'May I have?' / instead of 'Give me.'"

"That was hot."

"Today is about you, to get to know you."

"I can't compete with that. I smoke maybe once or twice a week, sometimes not at all."

"The only good thing about it was that it was only weed. I know some people who moved on to harder shit from that pattern I just mentioned. Shit is real. The more I blaze, the more

I want to blaze. No expectations to do shit but get my lungs dirty. Then one day, I awoke. After tribulations, of course."

"What tribulations?"

"Damn, girl, I just confided in you with some personal shit. Didn't I tell you earlier to stop being a listening junkie? Now it's your turn to paint a picture of your upbringing."

"Well, since you shared something personal, I guess I have no choice, right?"

"I'm ear-hustling now."

"This stays at this bar. I used to be a man."

"What? Stop playing."

"I just wanted to see your face. Seriously, I was the typical silver spoon girl. I never wanted anything. Had everything. During my freshman year in high school, I decided to join the cheerleading team. When I met the leader of the football team, the quarterback, Marcus, I mean, it was love at first sight."

"Spend the rest of your life with him at first pipe?"

"Let me finish, Arthur."

"Go on."

"I gave him something priceless. One time we were fooling around, making out."

"Sorry, but you sound like a white girl. Who the hell says 'making out'? Where are you from?"

"Are you going to let me finish?"

"After convincing me to take the other half of this pill, that led to my own pill. The sex was out of this world. Anyway, I became pregnant with my first child. Two months and one week later, he gets killed. That left me to be a single mother. When I left home, my relationship with my parents was off course. I dropped out of school. I had an abortion. I guess losing two loves was just too much. I just wanted to be with him wherever he was, even past the green pasture. I just tried to end it all.

With his gun. He had it in the top drawer at our apartment. Thank God I didn't know much about guns, because I had the barrel in my mouth but the trigger did not move. That's the only thing that saved my life, not knowing the safety was on. I must've sat there for maybe an hour trying to get the gun to go off. I got frustrated and threw the thing across the room. That's when it went off and scared the living daylights out of me. I swear to God, I saw a ghost image of him staring right at me at that moment. I rely on God in every situation in my life, good or bad. No matter what. I know he will see me through. Happy now, Artie?"

"Malaysia don't cry. It's OK. You were a gun virgin for a reason."

"You know how to make me smile, don't you?"

"My duty is to please the booty. I'm stealing a hug."

Chapter 7

Is Living and Dying a Lesson?

> For my hood, especially
> Rival crews and the PYTs,
> Baby mamas and their brand-new seeds,
> OGs, even the haters that wanna be like we,
> Twist backwards with regular weed,
> Sipping from a plastic cup,
> Violate you, pressing your luck.
>
> —Leery

"Yo, what's good?" Nitro asked.

"Listen, my nigger, these niggers had the drop. The victorious one became the victim, na mean?" Butta said.

"I will be there in a half. I will hit your phone when I touch down."

"Say no more."

Butta's phone rang twice before he picked up and was greeted by Nitro. "I am pulling onto the pavement now, Butta."

"What happened, son?"

"I was posted in the attic trying to bag this shit. That's when I heard unfamiliar voices. The first thing I assumed was that the boys had gotten us. Then I looked out the window. I didn't see any suspicious V's, so I grabbed my teenage life-ender, my Glock nineteen, and she got to work on these two niggers. They'd gotten too big for their britches. You see this nigger? The other one is over there to the right of the kitchen. What the fuck are we gonna do?"

"Just be easy. I got you, Butta. Butta, go get the work and cash. Hold up, where's Kiwi?"

"That nigger in the basement. Been asleep this whole time. He is a heavy sleeper. I think he got a condition or some shit." Nitro made his way to the basement.

"Yo, Nitro," Kiwi said, before Nitro put three bullets in his head and returned to the top level. Butta returned from the attic with his black and yellow duffle bag full of items. As soon as he turned his head and walked to the door, Nitro repeated his actions, putting the Glock to the right side of his head and blowing his brains out. Underworld dealings.

*

Funerals are always dark, no matter what. Especially seeing the hurt of a family member. But nothing can compare to the sadness on a mother's face. The four of us paid our respects. But the uncomfortable part for us all was that this was number one of two funerals, close together. The Grim Reaper had been busy as a motherfucker. Everybody must answer when God calls. We also had to pay our respects to Young Gunner. Hurt and pain. Should've, would've. But now it was too late to turn back the hands of time. I wasn't the only one who felt the tension from Stupid's kinsfolk. We made a move shortly after the walk-through.

Funeral number two reminded me of an old public-school assembly. This from a person who'd hardly gone to school. Seemed that the whole school was in attendance. Gang members with whom Stupid had had ties indeed made their presence known. As his mother, his baby mama, and his little sister competed for a plaque for the most terrible reaction, I couldn't help but shed a tear.

We spotted Tracey and Malaysia, who hadn't known Gunner very well but who paid their respects, nonetheless. The tears running down their faces made their makeup run. They resembled witches, but pretty ones—and they looked sexy as hell in their outfits.

Since the girls had shown up, we were going to go sip something and fog up the sky. Deciding to cipher the shit up, we made an executive decision to head to Malaysia's crib. Since she was certified in putting it down, we figured the grub would be on point.

The women stopped at the liquor store to get some Hennessy VSOP. We matched their purchase.

Back at the crib, we began camouflaging the pain we had witnessed in the funeral today. Seemed like the right thing to do. From session to session, the painting of soulful pictures of Stupid Face and Young Gunner had everyone a bit depressed. Before the L's and them liqs, which had us celebrating their homecoming. We knew that they were present at that particular moment. We had gained two angels.

"Yo, look at this, Red snoring with his mouth open."

"I should smack the shit out this nigger and wake him up to see his reaction," Blue said. Out of nowhere, Tracey and Malaysia started cracking up.

"Damn, this nigger got saliva dripping down his chin," Tracey added. "He probably can't handle the Henny, like P.P."

"What the fuck is you talking about? I was in a zone of my own till I heard the snoring," P.P. said.

"Red, go lay down in my room. Your ass high like a kite," Malaysia said.

"No doubt. Wake me up in an hour before you disappear."

"That good weed mixed with the Hennessy is a remedy for back breaking, and eyes don't lie."

"P.P.?"

"What, Tracey?"

"You look like you over there in the zone. What you thinking about, some new pussy?"

"Sex rehabs can't help him," I said. "Why you laughing, Tracey?"

"You got mirrors in your pants. I see myself in them."

"You look like you need your wall redecorated. I guess I fit the description of the man who can do it. I read your mind, Tracey. Come sit over here."

"You come over here, nigger."

"Man, listen."

"Shut up. You hear that, P.P.?"

"That sounds like my man Blue, stretching her insides."

"That's what we should be doing."

"I wouldn't mind."

Tracey and I started lip-locking, and that led to my gently patting her curves down like the police. And that led to my gently pressing my tool into her without a tee. Lust had taken control of me. If it was wrong, then I didn't want to be right. The episode lasted about twenty minutes. Her vise-grip pussy had me contemplating the possibility of my offspring's going swimming too late. I became a victim of lustful circumstances.

*

Sasha explained the recent events to her best friend. Mariann could not believe what had transpired.

"Godspeed. May you overcome the tragedy and return to everyday life."

Mariann sat quietly and soaked up what her best friend tried to explain through tears. Focusing on her hurting friend suddenly brought a stream of tears to her own eyes. Mariann decided to exit the room, only to return in less than thirty seconds with a small Ziploc bag of high-grade marijuana and some crumbled fronto leaf she'd gotten from one of her trick-and-treat friends. She knew that her friend needed to smoke so that the grief would stop disturbing her peace, if only for a moment. Only people who blazed would understand that move. The look in Sasha's eyes told Mariann a story that outside people would never understand.

Soon they could smell the aroma of fine grass. The good weed put Sasha in a chatting mood.

"Just when I put my guard down and let a nigger in. Shit never works out. Why can't I leave this life and live a normal life? I finally found a square dude who adores me and respects me."

"Don't start the waterworks again," Mariann said. "I've sat and listened to you reminisce about your past good times like J.J. and Thelma. But you need to live for him instead of crying for him. That is what he would want you to do."

Mariann sat beside Sasha and tried her best to console her. When their eyes met, green wasn't the only thing that sparked.

Their lips locked. They started caressing each other's breasts, then moved below the hips. Slowly, they removed each other's garments, each of them trying to out freak the other, nibbling on each other's paradise. Sasha's moaning sounded lovely to Mariann. Tears of hurt had turned to tears of joy. As Sasha's body started to cave, Mariann held her in place as Sasha embraced the oral pleasure. All Sasha could do was shake gently and uncontrollably until she felt that intense feeling of satisfaction subsides.

Sasha sucked her juices from her bestie's lips with ease. They held each other as if they were one person without uttering any words. The silence was broken when Mariann greeted a caller on the other end of the line. The "hello" greeting led to a surprising choice of words she had not been expecting. Not knowing the caliber of problems that were ahead, Mariann was stunned, but she dismissed the caller as a hater lacking the means to remix a memorable episode.

Chapter 8

A Broke Bastard with Potential

I roll dolo from state to state,
Focusing on cake. Reaching my destination, I
Can't wait. I'm on the hound.
Vacate so them boys don't hound.
Cover new ground. Head nod
Instead of a pound. Love and hate
In every town. My product is raw, pure.
Money got me head over heels like Allure.
It crosses my mind like Jill. Shit
Going wrong. Might have to bang a hater with the
steel I'm trying to chill.

—Leery

"Yo, you think people will mind if we blaze with the dead?" I asked.

"Son, I am getting my lungs dirty for my nigger Stupid Face regardless," Blue uttered. "Like my nigger Leery said, I'd blow the smoke in the air, but the deceased is already high up, watching over." He blew smoke rings with his mouth.

"Nobody got the blicker, right?"

"Some motherfuckers wanna call the cops, doing Jake's favors and shit."

"A fine or bullpen therapy is worth my nigger getting his lungs dirty in this cipher with us for old time's sake," I said.

"Puff, puff, pass, Blue. Motherfucker acts like he's on a dolo mission. Ricky Steamboat–ass nigger. Two middle fingers and my middle toe, nigger."

"I'm gonna mourn my nigger Stupid Face until I join him. Straight cheese," Black said. "Who the fuck rolling to V-A with me? I should try to dent Lucy's insides out there."

"I know P.P. ain't talking. I heard about you eating ass like groceries, and we are still passing the smoke to this nigger."

"Fuck out of here. Don't listen to shit that Black Turtle over there says. Yo, Black Tar, baby, it did not go down like that."

"Whatever, nigger. I heard some other shit, but I'm keeping it on the down-low. That's nothing compared to using your lips as toilet paper," Blue said.

"Nigger, I washed her ass, I mean."

"What?"

"Yo, Red, take the blunt from this nigger. No more blazing with this dude. He is now banned from ciphers for life."

"So, that's that man's issue?" Red said.

"Damn, another ass-eating representative," Blue uttered.

"Black, when are you planning to take your small fortune stakeout?" Red asked with smoke in his lungs.

"Lucy said I should roll this weekend for spring break."

"Lucy? Y'all keep in touch like that?" Blue asked.

"Shorty was stressing about quality and bullshit quantity. Big said Nicks went for twenties down south," Black sang while passing the blunt back. "I'm traveling light. If shit looks marvelous, it's on and popping. Lucy put me on. Damn near the whole school fuck around and needs some new lungs. So, imagine how we can corner the market."

"Slow down, Duke. Test the waters first. Then you can stack your brie. But all jokes aside, my nigger Omar lives down there. I don't know about the location, 'cause I never asked. He's probably a joint-rolling, dick-in-the-butt ass nigger. I think he works for one of those Fortune 500 companies. I don't know which one. If shit is official like a referee, shit is going to get real foul for the competition. Firmly. Just like my nigger Leery said, 'Organization accumulation got thinner pockets hating.' Believe it or not, Omar wanted to do some shit like this. But I assume he was just making conversation. He's shook since them niggers put a hole in him for running up in that discount store on the bully."

"How long have you known him?" P.P. asked.

"Like twelve years. Why?"

"If you can trust your son, that is a plus. He could hook you up with a camouflage job, and you'd be set, actual shit. In the meantime, be patient. Like Steve Austin says, that's the bottom line."

Five days later, Black took the E train to Forty-Second Street, heading to the Port Authority. His destination was West Virginia for spring break. Cool as a cucumber, with fifty nickel bags of New York's best rolled in a Ziploc bag, which was right in his 7-Eleven Big Gulp cup filled with ice water, Black went straight to the booth for directions and the departure time. He retrieved his ticket and went straight to the bus to get a seat in the back. A seat right next to the bathroom was sufficient as long as nobody dropped a bomb in that shit. Black figured he could calm his nerves as the bus made its moves. If you knew him, you could tell he was shaken up as if he had a trunkful of raw.

Black hit the restroom to blaze a little clip to ease his nervousness. After almost burning his fingertips off, he was back at his seat, smelling like too many sprays of cologne mixed with Febreze. He had sprayed the restroom like a madman to hide the smell in the small-ass room. Now he began reminiscing about his closest confidante, whom he would never again see in person.

It was totally silent as the pack piled into Baby's Blue whip. The Honeycomb was the destination, a new strip club that was getting a lot of ghetto reviews. Red, Cashout, Blue, and me, P.P., proceeded to empty our different cigars so we could restuff them. Cashout broke apart the lime-green branches and rolled several blunts. No one spoke a word.

"Black always told me this was some shit," Blue said while steaming the chronic. "Speak of the devil, this nigger must have touched down. Speak to me." Blue spoke over the music. "Put the phone on speaker. What is it? Yo, how shorty look?"

"I haven't met her yet. I'm still on the bus. That's what's up. Where is everybody?"

"Right here. You are on speakerphone."

"All y'all are bitch-made. Nobody rolled with a nigger. It's cool, though. Stupid would have been on the bus right beside me. Fuck all y'all niggers. I'm a holler. One."

Fresh off the bus, smelling like half a bottle of cologne, Black decided to light a cancer stick. "These Newports give me the shakes," he said to no one but the fresh air he was breathing. After a call to the homeys to see what was happening in the hood, informing them that he was about to hit the pavement, Black eyed the unfamiliar town. He was kind of lost, but he remembered Lucy's email, putting him in to the cheapest hotel to lie up in for the weekend. Just his luck, the hotel was not within walking distance of the bus terminal. "The Quality Inn on Northampton Boulevard," Black told the cab driver. The driver was so fat that he damn near took up both front seats.

"What's the price? And fuck the cost," Black said, frightening the cab driver.

"Nine dollars," the cab driver answered.

Once at his destination, Black paid the price for the ride, collected his change, and slammed the door. He began examining the crowd, realizing Lucy was a fucking angel for making reservations. He would have been assed out.

Black made his way to the reception desk, where he was greeted by a pretty Arab woman.

"Would you prefer smoking or nonsmoking?"

"That's how you do it down here? They don't ask that shit in New York," Black said loudly. He showed his ID in exchange for two key cards, then kept moving to his temporary place of rest. A hot shower was in order.

Forty minutes later, just like she had promised, Lucy was hood-banging on the hotel door like the Quality Inn was the projects. "Shanaynay, oh my goodness," Black stated, before snatching her off her feet and wrapping her in a loving bear hug. Startled for a moment, Lucy planted her feet back on the ground. "What are they feeding you out here? You thickened up in all the right places. You look like a showstopper, girl."

"Thank you."

"Are you ready to get your lungs filthy?"

"For sure."

"Roll this up."

"Fuck out of here. You handle that shit." Lucy gently separated the cigar while watching Black get dressed with lust in her eyes.

"What's going on with your amigos out there?" Lucy asked to make small talk. She was already aware of the recent events, having been keeping in regular touch with her girls.

"How do they treat you down here? It sure isn't slicing the Big Apple."

"Same shit, different toilet." Lucy released the smoke through her nose like her fellow smokaholic, then passed the little bastard to Black.

"What kind of work do you do?"

"I'm a receptionist at a medical practice, part time. Until my graduation this year, when I'll start making some real guap."

"I hear that, hot shit." Black nodded with admiration.

"Well, after I pay all these loans and credit card bills, I'll be making some greenbacks."

"What made you want to just break fast, like flapjacks and bacon?"

Lucy couldn't help but laugh at the way Black stated the question. "I just needed a change of scenery to focus on my future."

"The last time I checked, we had a shitload of colleges in New York."

"Sometimes you have to get away. But it does feel funny being alone out here, starting fresh. But, man, listen, I've got one year to go before graduation. With my master's in sociology, I could not be prouder of myself and my accomplishments."

"I hear you, shorty. I see where you are going with it."

"I hate that shorty shit. All these guys who try to holler 'shorty this' and 'shorty that.' I can't stand when people say that shit."

"Point taken, bitch. I'm just fucking with you."

"If a nigger ain't got at least an MBA, he can't even get a thorough conversation."

"Thank you."

"For what?"

"Saving me the embarrassment."

"Shut up. You know what I mean."

"I damn sure do. On a serious note, here is some food for thought. The same cat who approaches with that shorty shit is your mirror. Nine times out of ten, they say the same shit. Don't walk away from a divine connection."

"I hear you, B."

"Where do you lay your head?"

"Downtown Norfolk."

"That's near Virginia Beach?"

"Somewhat."

"I hear it's popping in Virginia Beach and Richmond."

"True shit. Let me warn you, it is not sweet out here. Motherfuckers get it in."

"You ain't gotta explain shit. Didn't I just say I hear niggers get it cracking? I'm lightweight right now. After this weekend, I'm gone with the wind like in the movie."

"I feel you. Just remember my words if you decide to rain on the competition like a shower."

"So, Lucy, what's on the agenda for this evening?"

"Just get in the car."

"Demanding. I like that, only when y'all are in your birthday suits. Where are we going? To hell with gasoline draws."

"We are not going to need any matches, but it might be hard to roll an L with all the heat. We're going to need some frozen water. I know you got them munchies."

"You are probably right.

"You get rap radio stations out this bitch?"

"Please tell me that was a rhetorical question. How are we not going to have rap stations? We are not in some Third World country. They got rap music over there too. Most likely."

"All right, point taken. You had to go into speech mode. All that ass had to do was switch that shit to the channel. Turn that shit the fuck up, if you don't mind." Lucy revealed a smile before conquering the task. Black sparked a new L and took a few tokes before passing it to Lucy.

"I know you are leaving me with some of this, right?"

"I got you. You ain't have to say a word." Black made a mental note of her last statement. She was a smokaholic just like he was.

Back at Shorty's crib, Black made himself at home while Lucy showered. He wanted to join her, but after the convo at the hotel, he understood it was not happening unless she initiated the episode. The munchies got the best of Black and had him snooping through the fridge for some snacks.

Lucy walked up behind him and screamed at him, "Get your ass out of my fridge!" That shook his ass up. "How do I look?" she asked, giving him a supermodel spin so he could take in what she had on: a one-piece money-green wraparound that perfectly enhanced her curves.

"Even better. Not too much on display, but you are killing them with the round bubble."

"I'll take that as a ghetto-as-hell compliment," Lucy replied with a smile.

"Word to everyone I love. That scent got my dick hard like Chinese trigonometry." Lucy's laughter almost brought her to tears.

"I got some three-cheese ravioli in the freezer."

"Hook that shit up before I do, good looks."

"I got you."

"Do you want crackers or garlic bread?"

"Garlic bread, if you don't mind."

"Not at all. The club should be popping by the time we eat and bullshit a little bit. We might stop at this house party. I promised them a walk-through to say hello. After that, we can get our groove on at the club." Black and Lucy headed to her car, looking like a flashy young urban couple.

"Shotgun."

"You act like it's more than the two of us heading to the vehicle." Lucy smirked and shook her head. "You ain't never going to change."

"For sure, I'm the same old g, from Lee's to acid-washed jeans." They placed their seat belts on as if they were in a race. Lucy was victorious. Black proceeded to roll a blunt. "You don't mind, do you?"

"Puff, puff, pass," Lucy replied with a grin. As the smell saturated everything from their outfits to the car interior, they both got their minds right. It was silent for most of the car trip before Lucy asked a question, snapping Black out of his zone.

"What's on your mind, Black?"

"Real shit, no perjury? Partin' your thighs at the end of the night."

"Shut up," Lucy replied, but she gave him a look that said she had considered that herself. Lucy parallel-parked alongside a Toyota TL, gliding into the spot skillfully.

"You are such a textbook student," Black said with his lungs full, causing Lucy to grin once again. Black hopped out of the whip like a detective about to pat down the nickel-and-dimers on the bully before accompanying Lucy into the house.

They were thumping that new Clipse joint, "Grindin'." "Grindin'. You know what I keep in the lining. Niggas better stay in line when you see a dude like me shining." Black couldn't help but sing along. That song's energy mimicked how he was feeling at the time, like he was back in New York with more people than should have been allowed at a crowded-ass house party.

Lucy introduced Black to her people. Maxine had some thick-ass thighs. Black extended his hand and smiled while introducing himself like a proper gangster and gentleman at the same time. With lust in his eyes, he repeated his greeting to Margaret.

Margaret put white women with an ass on the map with all her ass. Talk about booty. Her shit was all over the place. Black shook hands and headed straight to the get-wasted section. "A cranberry and Jack Daniel's," Black told the mixologist, before receiving his beverage. Lucy had disappeared, leaving Black and Margaret to get to know each other. Just as Black was going in for the kill with his New York swagger, some diesel dude grabbed her from behind and planted kisses on her neck. That move let Black know she was off-limits.

"Black, this is Aaron. Aaron, this is Black, Lucy's friend from New York."

"Nice to meet you."

The muscular man looked fit on top, but his legs looked wobbly as if they were having trouble keeping his body up. As soon as Black's jam began, he looked and saw Lucy approaching, looking like a model, he grabbed her and took her out to the dance floor, where he put a little twist on the two-step. Black whispered in Lucy's ear, making her blush.

"I love the way your hips sway, Lucy," Black said, staying on beat with his two-step. He became a bit aroused. Lucy sensed his arousal and had the nerve to grind a bit harder.

Black had no choice but to fall back and adjust his third leg's position. "Maybe you already considered that," he said in Lucy's ear.

"Maybe," Lucy replied with a slight grin. Funny, she knew what Black was insinuating. Lucy vanished again.

Having to drain the weasel, Black asked somebody where the restroom was. On his stroll back to the get-wasted section, he got Lucy a beer—nothing too hard since she was driving. As Black made his way through the crowd, he swung his arms to get by, frequently uttering, "Pardon me" and "Excuse me." He managed to knock down a drink that wobbly legs Aaron was holding. Black apologized and offered to replenish his yak. Aaron, being a prick, tried to start a confrontation. Black, with his New York roots, was able to detect the drama about to unfold. He asked what Aaron was drinking, but the guy was still using disrespectful gestures.

Scanning his surroundings for Lucy, but unable to find her, Black decided to get a breath of oxygen. As soon as he got his body out the door, Aaron and company came out, having followed him.

"It is always some bullshit," Black told the fresh air outdoors. Given the fact that he had offered to replace the drink, he figured the beef was not about the spilled yak. Wobbly Legs was just being a penis. Black walked away. Aaron threw a straight roundhouse to the side of his head. The blow caused Black to stumble and drop his drink. Then Black lost it. He pounded the dude for about one and a half minutes. Five other dudes came to Aaron's rescue and beat Black as if he'd stolen something, knocking one of his teeth out and severely bruising his face. Black tried to make a run for the car but was unsuccessful for more than one reason. The assault came to a halt as the guys regained their composure. All the spectators enjoyed the show until the end. Lucy and Maxine sprinted outside to catch a glimpse of the culprits.

"Oh my God, are you OK?" Lucy asked with sincerity.

Black could hardly move. "It feels like my ribs are cracked or bruised," he said.

Lucy dialed 911 and gave them the location. Then she helped Black to the car. Lucy opened her glove compartment for her small first aid kit, an excellent thing to have in an emergency. Black spotted her black-handled Glock 26. She tried to snatch it away from him, but to no avail. Black examined it like a gunsmith.

"Don't do anything stupid," Lucy said, which sounded more like a cry than a demand. Black took a puff of the blunt. As he heard voices getting closer, he spotted Aaron, who was still wasted. Walking closer, Black sat in the passenger's seat of Lucy's vehicle. As Aaron and company made eye contact with Black, he took a puff of the blunt and let the trigger fly. The entire group scattered for cover.

Black contemplated emptying the whole clip, but thought twice. Soon, paramedics and cops arrived at the scene. Lucy couldn't believe what had just gone down right before her eyes, but she was able to snatch the gun and return it to the glove compartment. All the spectators pointed their fingers at the car that Lucy and Black were sitting in, awaiting medical help. The paramedics assisted male who had multiple gunshot wounds to the face. Lucy helped the paramedics examine Black. He was more hurt than it seemed as the second truck arrived.

Black was handcuffed to a gurney and taken to the hospital for treatment and observation. This had been an unpredictable turn of events. Lucy followed the ambulance to the hospital, still unsure what would happen to Black.

Chapter 9

Veni, Vidi, Amavi (We Came, We Saw, We Loved)

> Blazing up with the crew, sipping Johnnie Walker
> Blue and cherry Pepsi,
> I got a call from a PYT,
> Said she was ready to let me
> Dig out her gut. I told her, "Shut the fuck up."
> Hopped in a cab. Gave her my honeycomb math.
> She said, "Give me an hour." She had to take a bath.
> At last, I'ma wax that ass.
> I hope I don't nut fast.
> I should rub one out. Nah, I'm a save the first set
> of offspring for her mouth, then I'm a wear it out.
> —Leery

Ever since the funeral, Tracey and I had been inseparable. She had me stuck, but I definitely had her in my web. There I was, sitting alone now, waiting for my divine gift to arrive. I was two sips away from being an alcoholic. When I heard the key unlocking the door, a ray of sunshine stepped into the room with her pearly whites on display. "Looking pretty ass all outdoors, but her stomach was round like an elementary school classroom globe, the type that sits on the teacher's file cabinet. I quickly rushed to the door to free her hands from the bags. It seemed that everybody was always giving her their old items, as if we weren't going to get a new version of this same shit at the baby shower. I was happy like a faggot in Boys' Town myself. My baby was about to have my baby. I was hoping for a boy, but if it turned out to be a girl, God might try to get me back for breaking young women's hearts.

I couldn't possibly find the right words to confront Tracey with my assumption—better yet, a guarantee—that she was most likely my daughter. I could see the resemblance in the pictures in her wallet, never mind the confrontation I'd had with Yaritza, the other half who had assisted me in the process of procreating. How in the hell would I even start a conversation like that? "I love you, and oh yeah, you might be related to me in a crazy way. How about I explain after God's gift is born?"

Maybe I wouldn't say shit at all. *Damn, damn, damn. Like J. J.'s mom, I need another bottle of yak. A brand-new seed, I need to leave that shit alone. What would Jesus do in a scenario like this? I mean, we are already in love, with a baby on the way. I can't even call it. I wonder, like Stevie, how she's gonna react to this shit I'm about to invade her space with. I knew this was too good to be true. We clicked like hips from day one. I was always her orange soda in the hood, her crush. She's got booty, brains, and beauty—triple B's. I mean, this is my daughter. How can I continue to dent her insides? I feel strange now just thinking about it. I wish I could just go take a nap, then wake up and find that this crazy soap opera shit is just a dream. Maybe I need to blaze some green to escape reality. But damn, I'm so addicted to the abnormal that reality seems strange. I can't lie. I was infatuated with her from day one. With a nickname like Peep Plots, Purchase Pussy, how in the hell did I not see this shit in a premonition?*

*

Living in a fog
Had me stuck
And unaware. Not seeing
Beforehand should
Be my biggest fear. A blessing
For those in the essence inside.
I shed a tear, apologize
To the ones who love me.
And I ain't really care. Now they don't really care.
Scarred.
Keep ya faith in God. Just believe that the things
you go through make you
Hercules, Hercules.

*

    How could I explain? Why couldn't she hop on my magic stick after she ate? I never saw this shit coming. It was too late for an abortion. But my abortion theory would be out the window if she decided to give birth. Damn, that ass had gotten fatter too. She got it from her mama. *Damn, there I go looking at the shit with the wrong head.* I used to hate that riddle. Men are from Mars; women are from Venus. Women think with their hearts; guys think with their penis. Actual shit, I can't lie. I promised I'd never hurt her heart, but this could possibly bruise it. Either way, I needed her and wanted her in my life. I knew it looked fucked up. *But let's just make the best of a bad situation.*
    Maybe I should say that. Yeah, I'll spit it out like that.
    "Tracey, we need to have a conversation."
    "Speak up. The floor is yours. I hope you ain't about to say you gay, or sick, or some shit like that."
    "Man, listen, miss me with that bullshit, bitch."

"What? You got five different baby mamas."

"Only three. I'm just joking. How's your mother doing?"

"Fine. Why do you ask?"

"Because I just wanted to be the first to tell you."

"Tell me what? You're scaring me. Just say what you are trying to say."

"It's not that easy to say shit like this. Your mother ever tell you who your father was?"

"Yes, some deadbeat sugar daddy. He had a sex addiction. He passed away when I was a baby."

"He didn't pass away. Listen, your mother and I were young. I mean really young. We shouldn't have been thinking about doing, let alone actually doing, what we were doing."

"What are you talking about?"

"Remember that Barbara Walters special on Channel Seven? This dude did some shit like that on purpose. That doesn't make me feel any different."

"Who the hell is Barbara Walters?"

"I really can't remember any details about the TV show. But it is similar to the *First 48* show."

"Oh, OK, that makes sense so far."

"Maybe that's why there's so much discrimination against people in the world to this day, people talking about keeping their bloodlines pure. Perhaps he had a good point, depending on how you see things and possibly what you have been through. That may explain some of the hate in people. The black-on-brown discrimination. Light-skinned people having problems with dark-skinned people. The short issue against the tall. Modern-day mind slaves. The good part is that I had no idea whatsoever when we were doing the nasty. Until I fell back and had to brainstorm."

"Wait, let me get this straight: you and my mom?"

"We were like nine and maybe eleven years old. It all started at the babysitter's house. We were playing in the backyard while the babysitter took care of us. One day we were running around and fighting. Do I have to go on?"

"Yes, you do."

"One day my little man, my third leg, was poking her, searching for an outlet to plug into—911. It was an emergency."

"What?"

"I can't remember those exact words. But that sowed a seed for us doing what we ain't had no business doing. Long story short, our trips to the backyard became auditions for our porn careers."

"OK."

"Get it now? Good, you are laughing. I thought your reaction would be different. I'm sorry I had to wait to tell you. I just could not muster up the right words. You have a baby. No, you have my baby. I didn't want to cause any heartaches. I made a promise to you that I would never hurt your heart. I apologize for this little dilemma."

"What. What little? I'm a big-ass damn house. Whatever you call it, it sure ain't little."

"So, what, you a cute mini-mansion?"

"I'm grown. But where do we go from here?"

"It is odd, but we still have to be in each other's lives, right, Tracey?"

"No, we don't have to, but I want to."

"Thank God. I thought you were going to break out like a rash or some shit. We got so much to handle. Tell your mother I said thank you for not telling you and giving me the opportunity to."

"Thank her yourself. That's your baby mama, right?"

"I see you got jokes."

*

"Two surf and turf on the fly," Executive Chef Malaysia ordered with authority, smirking and blowing a kiss in Arthur's direction. Arthur, the dramatic character, grabbed the kiss from thin air, turned his back, and wrapped his arms around himself as if he were in the midst of a passionate episode. Malaysia had to cover her mouth with her hand to stop herself from cracking up.

Nineteen minutes later, the two lobster and shrimp dishes were in the window, ready to go out. Malaysia examined the plates before the waiter could do what he got paid to do.

Officially an item, Malaysia and Arthur made the perfect team. They'd been friends before becoming lovers, and now they were lovers and friends. When life throws you a curveball, aim for the bleachers. Going on three years, six months, and fourteen days, the power couple loved to be in each other's company. Another large number of orders for the day kept them busy. But time flies when you're having fun. Arthur executed the garde-manger position with ease thanks to his mentor's insightful pointers, which put him ahead of the pack. Fucking the executive chef, Malaysia, sure did have its advantages. Arthur was a sure thing for the new sous chef position. The position was damn near his.

Malaysia ran the idea by him, and he was all for it.

"Hell yeah!" Arthur shouted a little too loud. But it was not official yet.

Chapter 10

No New Niggas

I'm in the hood with benefits.
Extra going hard.
You get the liqs;
I get the juice with my benefits card.
It all makes sense. Extra grimes on fire,
Niggers wearing wires, and they're liars. Spilling
the beans, they gas you up.
You ain't getting no cream.
Ya info ain't liable. Plus, I'm lying too.

—Leery

"Tie his motherfucking hands to his ankles!" Spare shouted to VD.

"Yo, what the fuck y'all doing?" Leery asked.

"This dirt-bomb nigger's benefit card is empty."

"So what?" said Leery.

"I gave this nigger a pass the whole week. This nigger wild in'," Blue laughed at crackhead Clifford, who was crying like it was his turn to meet his Maker, begging and pleading for Zone to stop his demonic antics.

"My social security check comes tomorrow," Clifford spit out between cries and pleas.

"I don't give a fuck. It's too late now, nigger." Just as Zone was getting ready to pistol whip him once again, a knock at the door interrupted Zone. Blue opened the door to find Jolly, Clifford's wife, standing there. She immediately handed Blue the money, which saved Clifford from an untimely demise.

Jolly managed to cop herself a few pieces, which she placed in her purse, before helping Clifford out of the spot he was in.

"A true fiend love story." Blue's laughter could be heard outside as he coughed his lungs out, holding a cancer stick. Just as Jolly was walking out the door, Stomp approached the gate.

"Back from foreign soil. My army comrade is home," Blue added.

"My nigger Stomp home," Zone said.

"You ain't got posttraumatic stress disorder or no shit like that, right? Shit gets hectic over there," Leery said.

"What's ya body count? I know you get paid to lay niggas like waves. That's what you do, right? What are your stats with the big joints y'all be holding?" Blue said.

"Is it true Uncle Sam giving niggers two seventy-five-hundred-dollar checks just for signing up for that shit?" Leery asked. Stomp just nodded in answer to the line of questions Leery asked, paying him no mind at all.

"I should've signed up for real. Real shit, no perjury," Zone said.

"What's up with them out-of-towners moving pure pearly white?" Stomp asked.

Stomp listened attentively to Blue as he spilled beans. Boot-to-Grill, a.k.a. Stomp, was a former service dude home on a dishonorable discharge, getting government cheese. Basically, he was in the hood with benefits. Stomp had an "I don't give a fuck about anybody or anything" attitude, including not giving a fuck about Blue, although he showed him some love, as if they were as close as brothers.

A Clearer Fate

"Stomp, since my people Stupid Face's untimely demise, I have not had a ride to the casket drop nigger."

"To help me multiply his currency, you are the perfect substitute, my dude."

"You look like we ride in the same zone like the cyclone," Blue said.

"Stomp, all we need is for them niggers to put us on their payroll. Then it'll be all she wrote."

"How the hell can that become a reality?"

Blue's questions caused Stomp to display his evil smirk, kind of like he was ahead of the line of questioning.

"Simple, my dude. We eliminate his soldiers. That way, he will need manpower. Like that camp I used to go to back in the early eighties."

Blue was silent, then began to laugh. "Damn, it is easy to see now," he said.

"Son, leave the proactive planning to me," Stomp said.

Boot-to-Grill, a.k.a. Stomp, mapped out a foolproof scheme. Blue and Stomp were ready to hop in the hooptie to smoke a few corner boys like looseys, infatuated by the kickback of the Uzi, but decided to call it a night. Blue made it his business to get with Stomp at a later date.

Chapter 11

Meanwhile, Back in the Hood

> Back in the hood. Smokaholic,
> So we twist another backward.
> Vodka or cognac in
> Vodka and orange-carrot mystic.
> This night should be uplifting,
> Terrific. Bust a few off. I ain't talking
> About the biscuit back to
> The crib like Jewel's and Chris
> Conversation like Ping-Pong,
> Back and forth, to
> Deep-throating my ding-dong in my zone.
> In every hood, probably the same song.
>
> —Leery

Nitro accompanied Tina to a cozy New Orleans restaurant. They wanted to pick each other's brains. It was a candlelight dinner with red wine and a lovable jazz band. The soft music massaged their eardrums. Tina was impressed with Nitro's mellow mood and unique restaurant choice. She seemed totally up for the brain-picking theatrics.

"Are you enjoying yourself?" Nitro spoke with finesse.

"It is a bit different scenery from what I'm used to," Tina said.

"Tell me what you're used to. Maybe I can arrange something. As a matter of fact, I don't know anything about you except for the digits you gave me. To have you embrace me with your beauty." Nitro caught her off guard with his compliment.

"Charming and handsome. OK, well, I'm a consultant. I live a high-maintenance lifestyle. A lot of men can't keep up with it. And I absolutely love fried chicken."

"I see you work out often. Your body's so firm," he said, complimenting Tina once again. "Fried chicken must agree with you."

"No, I work out seven days a week just to keep myself in tip-top shape. I also have a sweet tooth. Exercise is a must."

"My workout plan can make your backyard bigger."

"What? I have never heard that before," Tina replied with an indifferent look.

"Maybe later on I can show you," Nitro remarked, glancing at the menu. "I'm having a hard time staying in my seat. I can't help the urge to wrap my arm around you."

"Slow down, cowboy." Tina blushed. Nitro had images of sucking her up like a bowl of spicy gumbo. He slipped his hand into his left pocket to take out the money to cover the dinner. He left a generous tip before walking behind Tina to return to his place of rest.

"Nitro, it has been nearly three weeks since we last spoke. I thought you were no longer interested."

"Do I sense a bit of insecurity?"

"You are full of yourself, Nitro. But I love confidence."

"I know you do. It seems like I struck a nerve," Nitro replied boldly. He made a mental note as he pushed his vehicle toward a loft in Brooklyn, planning on spending a quiet evening with Tina and picking her brain a little more. Then he'd pick those pretty panties off.

LEERY

Tina sat in the passenger seat staring out the window with God knows what on her mind. Nitro parked the whip behind his E-Class Benz. He hopped out to open the door for Tina, just as he'd done when she first entered the vehicle. Once inside, Tina was impressed with the small but elegant loft. She made herself right at home.

*

Ever since Sasha had witnessed Jason's brains splattered on the glass window, she was never the same, including with her extracurricular activities. She'd even started carrying her quarter-water in her purse. She wasn't feeling the club scene like she used to. Her feelings for Jason were authentic. He was a square who had treated her like a queen. Not knowing if his killer lived by the old-school code of no women and no children, and leaving no witnesses behind, she had to go on with her life. She figured it would take a second for the grief to stop disturbing her peace.

Thursday at Daydreams was usually a good money night. All the city workers and older gentlemen had a thing for pretty young women. Sasha could use a lift in her stash. Her knight in shining armor no longer fit the bill.

Sasha dialed her girl to come pick her up. New money was just within arm's reach. Assuming she'd gotten her girl back 100 percent, Mariann kicked the gas once Sasha was in her V. Their small talk came to a halt when two dick-in-the-butt police officers, Pollutant and Bigbits, decided to pull them over for going thirty miles per hour in a twenty-five-mile-per-hour zone.

"No need for greetings. License and registration," Bigbits demanded.

"What is this inconvenience?" Mariann asked.

"Well, it seems you were speeding, going thirty miles per hour in a twenty-five-mile-per-hour zone. Where are you ladies off to?"

"Sorry, Officer, we just got a call from the doughnut shop. They only have four chocolate glazed left. It is an emergency."

"Keep it up," Officer Pollutant replied before storming back to the car. Finally, the officer returned with Mariann's license and registration and told the women to have a nice night.

"I can't stand them doughnut-eating motherfuckers," Mariann said, causing abrupt laughter from Sasha. Judging from the time, the two women figured that money was to be made. Both of them would be satisfied by the end of the night.

*

Hood Politic coughed up a lung from the Cali contraband that Stomp had passed. He was still blowing smoke rings when he heard his name being yelled out loud as hell. Typical hood shout-outs interrupted his train of thought. Hood P. gave Stomp a nod as Hood P. went to let Caramel in.

"About fucking time, nigga." That was Caramel's usual greeting.

"What's good, ma, with your sexy ass? Hold up, give me a runway spin. Let me soak all that in. It is a lot to embrace."

"Hop, skip with me to the deli real quick?" Caramel asked.

"Whatever," Hood Politic said. "Your butt cheeks got asthma in those jeans."

Caramel recognized the game and started laughing. Back at the tenement, Stomp waited for Hood P. to return. As Hood P. walked in and Caramel closed the door behind them, Stomp got a bird's-eye view of that ass in those jeans. With a thirsty stare and a smirk, he said, "That's paint. She had to butter her thighs to get them shits on."

I bet her butt cheeks are sweating right now. Her booty is having a hard time breathing right now, he thought.

"Do you like what you see?" Caramel's question had Stomp exactly where she needed him to be. "It's pay-to-play over here. We can do whatever you like." Stomp gave her a nod and rolled a new blunt, which he passed to Caramel. Caramel inhaled like the vet she was, then got up and handed it to Hood P. Caramel put some extra sway in her hips on her way back to her seat, knowing that Hood P.'s and Stomp's eyes were glued to her round roast. Her glance back at them confirmed her thoughts, and she smiled. Stomp reached and grabbed a big bottle of Bacardi Limon, a Caramel favorite. Her eyes twinkled.

Stomp went to the kitchen to get some cups and a one-liter bottle of Sprite. While Stomp was in the kitchen, Hood P. passed Caramel an Ecstasy pill, which she put in her mouth quicker than a blink.

Stomp returned with essentials and took the chronic back to his seat. Caramel proceeded to crack a Dutch Master down the middle to roll her special kind of cigar. She dipped in her purse and swiftly located a folded envelope containing a pearly white substance, with enough courtesy to ask if they minded if she sprinkled the weed with coke. Hood P. and Stomp didn't mind at all. She separated a few lines with a rare two-dollar bill. Snorting one line up her left nostril, she placed the other two in her L and twisted it up. Stomp poured himself and her another drink while Hood P. twisted some more green to keep the cipher complete. As the pill took effect on Caramel, she crawled on her knees toward Stomp, freed his third leg from his Hanes, and introduced her lips to his manhood. Not one complaint came from Stomp. Hood P. used that time to try unbuckling her pants to slide them down just to put baby oil on her booty.

"Seems like she is already wet," Hood said, sliding two fingers inside her to see how it smelled. She passed the Hood hygiene test with flying colors.

Stomp took his third leg out of his boxers and stuck it in Caramel's ass with no lube, just a little saliva on the tip of his tool. Caramel stopped her lip service to grind her hips back and forth before covering Stomp's top like a shirt. Stomp placed the L in the ashtray before grabbing her ears and rubbing his finger across her jawbone. Caramel seemed to be in a trance, putting in work on his microphone. Hood P. slid out of her so she could step out of her jeans. Caramel stood there, her booty looking like two big midgets behind her as she fingered herself. Stomp bent her over while Hood P. fucked her face. Aroused by her juicy-looking pussy, he placed the neck of the Bacardi bottle into her juicy fruit before sliding his tool into her ass. A fan of double penetration, Caramel grinded away and threw it back with a vengeance. Hood P. enjoyed the sloppy-toppy while lighting the L to steamboat for dolo. Mouth-to-ass hos on demand. Stomp and Hood Politic were huge fans.

*

"Stand up for the count, Big Head Ronald," the correction officer yelled out.

"Sucker-ass rent-a-cop, babysitting in the dormitory. He thinks he is the motherfucking man."

"Zone, yo, chill. He cool."

"Say I won't smack the shit out that nigger." Zone tried to get his man to cosign his bullshit.

"I dare you!" Wish yelled with a smirk on his face. Wish a nigga would have attempted to throw the battery in his homey's back.

"You think I won't? I give no fucks."

"Zone, you ain't about that life," Hammer said.

"Fuck is ya man talking about?" Zone said.

"Hammer, he bitch made, bleed for seven days. Wish a nigger would' said. This nigger wanna start a riot."

"It is possible he wants his ass busted," Hammer said. "Tell me what kind of sense that makes. Just imagine how much money they get for a nigger to stay in this motherfucker. Jail is big business. They love you. All you need are big shoes, a wig, and a big clown nose, clown-ass nigger. I see you do not get the big picture. I'll distance myself physically from you then. Bad enough that this pretty young thing caught me slippin'. It is a lesson in everything, my dude. Be humble. I probably ignored the signs, preoccupied with her thick-ass thighs. Her body was banging like Bloods and Crips. That ass and her bitties were swollen. I took the bait. She said she was nineteen. A big-ass youngin. I should have checked the bitch's age. My mistake. I really have to stop contemplating with the wrong head. That's what the fuck got me stuck in this place. That football dude LT caught a break; he got cake. I'm a broke bastard. I got priors like Richard. This bid I gotta face. Fuck it, a clearer fate."

"Damn, son, pretty young thing got that ass. Wish a nigger would' said."

"That's why I like older bitches. They don't give a fuck if you are married or single. We get it in, and she might let a nigger hold something, and I ain't gotta call her for weeks. See, if you find Jesus, he could hook you up with one of Mary's homegirls."

"Shut the fuck up, girlie-mouth-ass nigger."

A Clearer Fate

"Yo, Hammer, you think that bitch gonna come to court and all that?"

"Even if she doesn't, they're gonna jam that ass up. Like my nigger Leery said, 'The punk judge won't post no bail. / Stuck in a cell, one step above hell. / Somebody snitching, or I must have had a trail.'"

Chapter 12

Lord Knows

I got a fetish for knowledge.
I want to see how smart you is.
I be sure you are a genius if you swallow my kids.
Fine, gargle and spit.
Rub it on your tits.
Shorty's nice on my microphone. Yeah, it's a hit.

—Leery

Amid a hostage situation was not how I wanted to spend my morning. But my offspring were being held hostage. Monica was gonna be my hero and free my offspring. Maybe she was just in the mood. Perhaps she went to school. Maybe she was a mind reader. With that good brain. I was ready to take the bitch shopping. Word to everything I love. True story: no sooner did our romantic morning start than an urgent call came through. I almost ignored that shit. As a matter of fact, I would have, but my phone was within arm's reach.

"Yo, Leery, I need you to help me with this issue real quick."

"Dolla, I'm busy right now. I'm gonna have to hit you back. What the fuck is the deal?"

"Son, this bitch just violated."

"Who?"

"Baby mama."

A Clearer Fate

"My homey crying on the line like he bitch made, wifey found out he bicurious, go both ways. Went across his face with a switchblade."

"My dude, that sounds like family matters, like the Winslows. Anything but that. I will be quick to sin, though you on ya own."

"My nigga, no disrespect, but your baby mother got a fat ass. Talk to the tone." I hung the phone up, continued playing Bill, and let Monica do her job. Since she wasn't my bitch, my kids were all over the place. I called that foreign invasion. Thank the Lord for sluts and whores. Amen.

*

"How much paint does it take to get them jeans on?"

"Three-quarters of a can." Plumpness got to cut that ass out of those shits.

"Your offspring is with his grandmother. So nobody is here to keep us up bitching and crying. So, let's work on some siblings."

"Tracey, that sounds really, really good. But we can't do that anymore. You, of all people, should know and understand that."

"I know the circumstances are a little crazy, but we already smashed."

"We already what? Man, listen, Tracey, miss me with the bullshit. Hard as it is for me to resist, you want to throw it in my face. Get off my belt, Tracey!"

"I know you want to."

"Hell yeah, I want to. But since I'm 110 percent sure that, well, you know … What I'm trying to say … I have to struggle to resist."

"You don't have to."

"Yes I do. Right now, you don't understand, but soon you will. It's hard not to bend you over this couch and redecorate your walls."

"Yes! Yes!"

"No, no, we can't. We can, but we shouldn't, so we are not."

"You know what? It's cool. I'm OK with it."

"This is how it's going to be. Tracey, you comprehend?"

"No, but anyway."

"Don't be mad."

"About what?"

"Flap your wings, lovely butterfly. Sprout, but don't be stupid. What you are feeling right now will come and go on your journey. You better stand for something. It makes it harder to fall for anything. Everything that glitters ain't gold. Remember that."

"Whatever. I'm out of this joint."

"Where are you going, Tracey?"

"To mind my business, bitch-made-nigger."

I decided to have a chronic session. I needed to get my mind right. The comment "Don't get mad" kept replaying in my mind. I was a thinker. Sometimes people said I overanalyzed. I started to dwell on three different scenarios of what was ahead. Would it be heartache, disbelief, or just plain disrespect to the tenth power? Lord knows. As I rose, blowing the smoke through my nose, I realized I needed a new addiction. This weed got my dick hard like a brick. I suddenly visualized Tracey wriggling out her jeans and assuming the position. Just like that, I was ready to do the remix and purchase some pussy. I quickly dismissed that thought and decided to check Yaritza—Tracey's mom—and little man. I wondered if I could. "Your mom's got a phat ass. Just call me a motherfucker".

Chapter 13

It's the Unknown That Hits You the Hardest

You said I bruised your heart, crept in the dark,
Too many L's being sparked.
When I see you, don't even speak.
Shit, I'ma walk over you like the concrete.
I'm felony, bitch I build like Bellamy. Fuck what you telling me.

—Leery

When Cashout first laid his eyes on Tracey, he felt that it must be a clearer fate. Usually, a beautiful woman was the norm. But Tracey had niggers breaking their necks riding past in vehicles, damn near crashing, to get a second glance. That ass was visible no matter what she had on. She had two of his mandatory characteristics from the first look. There was only one way to find out the third. Cashout mimicked the scene in *The Wizard of Oz*. "If she only had a brain." With seconds to approach to drop his mack dosage shit, Cashout grabbed Tracey's hand, startling her.

"I have never seen one up close before," Cashout said.

"Seen what?"

"An angel. I had to make sure you were real. Don't you know angels are a rare breed in my society? I'm never letting go."

Tracey still couldn't read his intentions, but she dropped her guard a bit and smiled. Not even an hour after calling her baby daddy, bitch made, and all other shit under her breath. This new dude had changed her focus. She was intrigued by Cashout, his gift of gab. Tracey became a victim of his pimpology. Cashout wined and dined her, bought her all she desired, played the plumber and laid the pipe, listened to her and gave her advice, and even became a great father figure to P.P. Jr. at first. Cashout was able to paint her a Barbie and Ken fantasy. Penetrating through her mental walls, he removed any guard she had up.

Tracey was so into Cashout that she ignored the signs and the red flags, including the frequent calls from other women. She looked past the late nights out without question and even kept it to herself when he was away for days without any communication. One day she decided to speak up about these discrepancies. That was the first time Cashout felt she was out of pocket and needed some discipline.

It's always the unknown that hits you the hardest, the things you don't see even though the signs are there. Tracey assumed that was a onetime situation, hoping things would change and life could return as it once was. She suffered from Stockholm syndrome. Sometimes a person was just in love with the fact of being in love.

Tracey lay on the floor in the fetal position, praying the blows would stop. But maybe God couldn't hear. All she could muster up was, "How the hell did it come to this?" Cashout kept throwing blows like he was in some kind of trance, sparring with a punching bag. He was high on only God knows what. He continued his one-sided boxing match until he suddenly saw another opponent, P.P. Jr., who had come wobbling out of the room, following the noise.

"Why are you crying, Mommy?" P.P. Jr. asked.

Cashout took it upon himself to unleash the same venomous rage upon P.P. Jr. Tracey was in a world of pain but she gathered enough strength to toss her body over the young boy who had stumbled out of the room to check on her. Cashout's sinister smile resembled the Joker's. He was sipping on pimp juice. Tracey had a premonition of consoling her son while in a boatload of pain. Her father's words finally hit her like a ton of bricks. The change was mandatory. Tracey asked herself how love could be so unkind.

Chapter 14

Ain't No Pussy like New Pussy

Adidas [All day I dream about sex]. I was a fiend ever since.
I was a teen, infatuated.
When she bent over to lean, I nose-dove right in.
Strap it up and dive right in.
I get my Clarence Carter on 'cause I be strokin'.
Doody brown, ebony brown.
It's red bones and yellow bones now.
White chicks, Asians with chinky eyes,
Undressing them with my eyes,
Sizing up them thighs.

—Leery

Nitro gave Tory a call early in the afternoon since he didn't have any business to handle for a few days. Plus, he had awakened with a vision of her elephant booty riding cowgirl style up and down his shaft. Tory said hello with the bass in her voice that he remembered. It had come from all the shotguns she'd taken like a champion in the chronic sessions. But Nitro was not worrying about her raspy voice at this moment.

"You got time for me?" Nitro asked.

"Sure I do," Tory replied.

"You sound like one of the fellas," Nitro said.

A Clearer Fate

"Don't let my voice fool you. I can tell you know what you like."

"You ain't gotta explain shit. I'ma pick you up in a minute."

Nitro hung up the phone, then he showered and shaved. He stepped out with a crisp FUBU velour suit, some Nike ACG boots, and a new fitted white hat, having sprayed on some drop-the-panties cologne. He'd also snatched up a substantial amount of cash and his jewelry and kept it moving. He hopped into the whip to go meet horse booty.

When Nitro arrived, Tory approached his whip in a tan form-fitting one-piece dress made by Guess. It had her booty looking like it was struggling to breathe, highlighting all her curves to perfection. Her white Gucci sandals complemented her outfit out just right. She applied her lip liner, MAC makeup, and perfume, hoping to have Nitro on his knees saluting her third nipple.

Tory placed her horse booty on the butter-soft leather seat. She greeted Nitro with a hug and a peck on the cheek. "Where are we off to?"

"Moneymaking Manhattan is all the information you are getting."

"I love your sternness."

"Roll the window down. Clear your thoughts in the breeze," Nitro added.

He turned on WBLS when they announced the 5:00 p.m. departure. Checking his watch spoiled the surprise. The cruise was scheduled to depart from Pier 63 in a little more than forty-five minutes. Nitro was cutting it close, but he made it on time. Special guests like SWV, Toni Braxton, 3T, and Maxwell guaranteed that Nitro would have an entertaining evening.

"You sure know how to plan a perfect first date."

"I try to make you feel comfortable. What are you drinking?"

"I will have vodka spritzer."

"I will be right back," Nitro stated sternly to Tory.

Nitro briskly walked to the bar while Tory sang along to the first performer, Toni Braxton. Nitro felt that he had really scored some points with the cruise. Once he returned, he handed Tory her alcoholic beverage. They bopped their heads to Sisters With Voices, enjoying each other's company. After the cruise landed them back at Chelsea Pier, a hot meal was next.

"Let's go to the Olive Garden to get some food to soak up all that alcohol," Nitro suggested.

"Fine with me," Tory said.

Once they were shown to their table, Nitro pulled out the chair so Tory could sit. He noticed how her ass spread as she sat on the chair. He was ready to fly, wanting to skip the meal and head straight to the closest Waldorf Astoria, but kept his sudden urge to splurge to himself. The liquor loosened Tory up nicely. She decided that dinner was going to lead to breakfast. After dinner was over, so was Nitro's anticipation.

Tory woke up from her deep sleep to find an empty space on the other side of the bed. She hopped out of the sack to place her huge booty on the toilet seat and relieved her bladder. She reached over to brush her ass-and-ball breath before eyeing the dresser with disappointment.

Nitro, you cheap bastard! she thought, before tossing the two hundred dollars in her purse. Tory grabbed her cell phone with frustration and dialed his number, but just as she had thought, he didn't answer. She placed a call to the front desk; she had forty minutes before checkout. Tory realized that her body was sore from last night, she squeezed her monstrous booty back into her attire and headed home for a nice soothing bath.

Chapter 15

Make Her Mind

> I don't love them.
> I don't hate them either.
> It's gotta be a trap. Who sent cha,
> Fate or hate? To the facts I was blind.
> Infatuated. Damn, I gotta make her mind.
>
> —Leery

"Round booty bouncing on my lap. No longer my comfort zone, matter of fact. Realistic premonition—why I'm sipping on this yak," Cashout uttered loudly. While sipping on his glass of brown water, he flicked the ashes from the blunt into the ashtray. As he was listening to the DJ spinning that new Leery joint "Make Her Mind," Caramel walked to the table and placed nearly three hundred dollars in big and small bills in his lap. Then she vanished under the strobe lights. Caramel was just one among his stable of go-getters. Standing at five foot five, she had a round booty and a nice cinnamon-sugar complexion. She would earn more money before the night was over. Then there was Chocolate, a.k.a. Big Booty Keisha. She happened to be Cashout's breadwinner. She had the biggest booty and the biggest bitties for her five-foot-nine height. But what kept the tricks out at night and the currency flowing was that she was as pretty as a mermaid. Shorty was killing 'em.

Tracey was a young bitch who put in her application as a bitch you had to have. She got hired on the spot. She was yellow-boned, maybe tan in complexion. She was semipetite, but her ass was fat. She had a body that could make a nigger wanna eat it. Official like a referee. She was also a natural beauty, no makeup—the type you wanted to sleep with every night, the type you needed in your life. Schooled to the duty. A tricking nigger weakness. She never was yours and never will be, but you wanted to keep her. Seasoned highly by others, Tracey, it seemed, had found her calling.

Club Passion was hot like a slave ship. Too many black bodies attracted heat. The place smelled like orgies and dirty money. On Tasty Thursdays, all transit workers and bus drivers got in for half price with a glance at their city ID cards. That was more money to throw at clapping ass cheeks until the day came. Women with irresistible figures strutted back and forth all night long, Lionel Richie style, counting currency for fantasies that could possibly come true. Old-school and new-school players alike were giving money away as if it grew on trees, throwing the bills to women who matched their shade of choice. Among the clientele were older dudes with handkerchiefs and gangbangers flagging, all of them with one thing on their minds at the end of the night: sweatbox stabbing. As usual, Tracey and her crew had them fiending. Caramel raked in the doe. Keisha's method was just to rope them in and keep them going back to the ATM to replenish their funds. A big booty and a smile had that effect. Seductive Tracey had niggers wanting to run away with her and have some babies because she gave the young ballers the business.

As Jeremy approached Tracey, making his way through the crowd of tricks and treats, the music switched to another tune. Money exchanged hands.

Tracey was on her way to whet her Adam's apple. Porkin Bean approached the bar. "Can I buy you a drink?"

"Yes," Tracey agreed. But her eyes were glued to the ground just like that night her mother let him steal her innocence. She was OK with him being that close. Jeremy passed her the drink she had ordered. Tracey took two sips and smiled. For some reason, she blushed. Older and wiser now, she saw an opportunity to accumulate some serious cash. Knowing a trick was always a trick, Tracey worked her magic. She knew that Porkin Bean liked to taste her banana cake. It had gotten sweeter with age, so she decided to charge him a hefty price to taste it again. The club started to clear out as the night ended. Without alerting her counterparts, Tracey began to make a smooth getaway.

Tracey and Porkin Bean Jeremy slid out the back door without missing a beat. Tracey sat back in PBJ's plush ride, telling herself she was in control. But her inner thighs told another story. Jeremy turned up his old-school McFadden & Whitehead. "Ain't No Stopping Us Now" blasted through the speakers. Tracey had a flashback about her body caving in when she was young. It was like a soul tattoo. *Anxious* was the only word to describe her demeanor at that moment.

"How have you been over the years?" Porkin Bean asked. "I knew you would be a star."

"What?" Tracey asked.

"You, a star. They can't get enough of you in that club. I am around and hear things."

"I ain't never see you there," Tracey said.

"You gotta be more aware of your surroundings."

It seemed that Jeremy transformed into another person as soon as he got behind closed doors. He strong-armed Tracey, similar to the first altercation, but this time with no restraints. PBJ's verbal assault controlled her percenter with no signs of easing up. His actions put Tracey in a deep sleep, which her body desperately needed. When she finally awoke, she felt brand new with an urge to please and to relieve her apple juice. She was prepared to eat breakfast with the person who sent chills down her spine from her younger day to the present.

Tracey ate quietly while listening to Jeremy explain his Pimping 101. She clearly understood what he was saying.

"I've never had sex with people watching me, let alone cameras watching," Tracey said to Porkin Bean.

"Don't worry, Tracey. Pretend you are alone with a trick who is making you wealthy."

"That's easier said than done," Tracey replied between bites.

Porkin Bean Jeremy and his partners were cofounders of the most successful porn company in Little Rock, Arkansas, Black Diamond Entertainment. They were also producers. Jeremy knew that Tracey would wow the industry with her natural beauty, her onion booty, and her natural ability to please. Plus, for some reason, he had a weakness for her fine ass.

In her first scene, she worked the camera like a professional. She was an instant hit, as if she had been waiting to explode onto the pornography scene. Shortly, she fell in love with the new lifestyle. Never once did she look back at the petty tricks and strip clubs. She was now touching more money than she had ever seen in her life, with plenty more coming from her new career. Jeremy's production company was getting calls from other companies to feature Tracey. She was thrilled. Jeremy declined the offers.

Tension was in the air because of the lack of expansion. One early afternoon, after a deadly assault on her pearl oyster, Jeremy decided to sit Tracey down and school her on the game because he had a soft spot for her.

Sparkle was Tracey's stage name as a porn star. She embraced the industry. Jeremy wouldn't let her stray too far and become a has-been from a popular name. Tracey loved the props, the camera tricks, and editing work. The porn scenes were stretched to last for hours so they'd make more money. Tracey wasn't aware that the industry grossed millions of dollars each year.

PBJ decided to fund Tracey's education. He didn't want her to go the route that many before her had gone, doing scenes just to survive or to support a habit, with no plans for the future. That way of operating made PBJ sick to his stomach. Tracey took his outlook into consideration. She trusted his judgment. Her enrollment in school satisfied his hunger more than the millions he had made in his career.

Chapter 16

Grimy

Mad different phases like mazes to find my way.
BK be the birthplace. Stop my shine.
These haters thirsty, man. Listen.
That's why I build and destroy.
Build like MacGyver. Each one teach one. I'm a hateful plot survivor.

—Leery

Arthur sat on the stoop with his man Hood Politic, coughing like an old-timer, he and Hood Politic passing the Godfather blunt back and forth. Now Hood was an old-school dude who had the best weed, hands down. You could smoke with Hood P. all the time, but you could not buy any of his stash from him. Plus, he would not tell you where he got his shit from. He was a funny-ass nigger. On top of that shit, Hood P. was the only dude who spoke the same phrase in many different ways.

As usual, Hood P. was barking at his female friend over the phone.

"Who gives a fuck? Kick rocks. Fuck out of here. Keep it gone." Sometimes I thought maybe he was making sure he got his point across.

"Trouble in paradise?" Arthur asked.

"You know, I keep it a hundred, stay good. I am holding my head, doing me."

"Baby mama bugging?"

"I told her I'm not the one, that's them other dudes, must be mistaking me. I handle my business, I step up to the plate, and you can count on me. I'm dedicated and determined. Bitch doesn't appreciate shit. I should have wrapped it up, put my helmet on, and magnified my tool."

"I feel you. Who was that brown-skinned chick with your baby mama earlier?" Arthur asked.

"You are talking about Felisha, hood rat, slut, ho, bitch, tramp. Trust me, you don't want those problems. That Stomp's piece. He can't get enough of that bitch."

"BTG?"

"You know Boot-to-Grill?"

"Yeah, he gets a nod. I don't fuck with him like I fuck with you, though."

*

Mariann couldn't explain her urge to smoke so much these days. But it had slipped her mind to pick up any paper to twist up with. Sasha, meanwhile, sat on her bestie's couch and separated her presidents, content that her stash was getting the face-lift it so desperately needed. She didn't budge. She made up her mind that she was not going with Mariann to the twenty-four-hour store.

"Damn, bitch, you can't walk with me?"

"You on ya own with that."

Mariann threw a mini tantrum but got dressed anyway and decided to carry her ass to the store alone. She slipped on her Nike running shoes, grabbed her keys, and power-walked up to the bully to handle her B.I. Frustration was written on her face, but what could she say to her bestie? Three people were waiting in line just to spend money in the wee hours of the night. Mariann was startled by the commotion of flashing lights and loud noises. The street pharmacist being harassed at his jobsite was nothing new. Finally, Mariann was able to retrieve her item, glad the wait was over. Snack options invaded her space.

"Let me get two packs of Drake's coconut cookies, five blunt wraps, and a bag of Cheetos." As Mariann dropped the ten dollars into the compartment beneath the cashier's window, a tall dude dressed in an NYC jacket, a Mitchell & Ness fitted hat, and some fresh Charles Barkley Nikes came and stood behind her.

"Excuse me, do you have the time?" Mariann ignored the question and walked away, passing the gentleman, who was next in line at the window, without uttering a response.

Mariann glanced back at the window as she opened her pack of cookies. She continued her stroll back home, never noticing the shadow on top of her own. Before she realized what was happening, a sharp object slashed across her face down to her neck. Mariann's cookies rolled up the block. Going in the same direction, the guy sprinted away into the shadows of the night. Pain, along with shock, invaded Mariann's space. The opening in her skin started to leak body fluid. Losing her senses for a few moments, Mariann just sat there and cried.

*

Lucy couldn't fathom what had taken place. She still blamed herself for what transpired. Her regret for having left him alone for a length of time haunted her. Maybe it could have been avoided. Black had asked her to get some answers from

A Clearer Fate

the police on his behalf. She realized that the outcome of the situation looked bleak. Lucy debated suggesting to Black that he consider a plea deal if one was offered. Black, being from New York, should have been aware of how things could turn out.

Even with a self-defense plea in this common law state, Black realized he might have to spend a little time in the big house. He might even be given a football number to make an example out of his black ass.

Black was still handcuffed to a bed in the hospital with a set of cops guarding him as if he were an important political figure. Finally, he got well enough to be placed in a holding cell. Like clockwork, the questions kept coming. Black exercised his Fifth Amendment rights and remained silent. A firm-walking, tall gentleman with a briefcase and slicked-back hair announced himself as Attorney Fairfield. The attorney noticed a blank, worrisome look plastered all over Black's face.

"Mr. Press, several witnesses are willing to testify. They heard and saw shots fired from the vehicle but could not see who exactly pulled the trigger, you or the female accomplice." Black couldn't believe his ears. Maybe he could convince Lucy to say she had pulled the trigger in an attempt to cover his own ass. The thought quickly vanished from his mind. Then he started to see things more clearly. He had pulled the trigger, not Lucy. Lucy was not locked up. He was the one who was going down, not Lucy.

"Lucy is a confidant."

"I am aware, Mr. Press. Lucy is the one who retained my services."

"My mistake. I had no idea."

"You do know that the gun is in Lucy's name and the car is in Lucy's name?" Mr. Fairfield added.

"Forensics proved that there were two sets of prints. Lucy will be subpoenaed to testify along with the initial witnesses. One last thing: the man who was shot, we lost him this morning." The lawyer had hit Black with bad news that could worsen things for him. "Your charge will be upgraded to premeditated manslaughter. Perhaps it could be reduced with a guilty plea. But like I said, I have to investigate further to give you the best-case scenario." The comment hit Black hard, like a punch from Ray Mercer. "Due to the victim's untimely demise, bail is out of the question."

Fairfield added, "I'll see you in court Friday. We'll talk before the court date in a few days."

*

Black sat still in court and listened to forensic discoveries all week. He heard witness testimonies that threw his ass under the bus. Friday came, and he was back in the courtroom waiting on the outcome. The deal on the table from the prosecutors, twenty years in prison, seemed like a lifetime to Black, so he figured to take a chance with a self-defense plea. But something didn't seem quite right as the deliverance from the court room got closer on the last day of the trial.

Lucy sat in the courtroom with a worried look on her face. At the court recess for lunch, she decided to have Greek food. As she exited the courthouse, a feeling that she was being watched snapped her back to reality. Now Lucy understood why Black's entourage from New York had not come to the trial. She could clearly feel the underhanded nature of how things operated.

Lucy said a silent prayer for Black while waiting in line for her lunch, which was taking forever. Ultimately, she had to take it to go. Back in court after having waited in the long line outside, Lucy sat on the aisle, embracing the deliverance. She sat there patiently and was not concerned about going to the restroom to relieve her bladder. Instead, she ignored the urge because she didn't want to miss the judge's final words.

Lucy was not surprised about the guilty verdict. But what made her empty her bladder onto the courtroom floor was the fact that the judge sentenced Black to sixty years. Black lost his balance; Lucy lost the fluid in her body.

The family of the victim applauded the verdict as if they were on a game show called *Seal That Motherfucker's Fate* and had won it all. Black's lawyer could appeal the ruling.

Chapter 17

Jezebel

> SFA [slut for authority] covers my top like a shirt.
> Knowledge is priceless, but
> Put a price on what it's worth.
> Certain episodes turn a warm heart
> Cold. I wonder what's worse, a hater who's distant
> or a hater who's close.
>
> —Leery

Tina spit on the tip of Polluten's penis before she deep-throated it, then stopped and coughed. She pleasured the officer skillfully while his partner, Officer Bigbits, waited his turn to get his knob polished. It was the clients who turned small hustlers into giants. Tina got well acquainted with the officers.

Thanks to her lifestyle, Tina's trifling ways backfired on her one lovely afternoon when her normal baller-milking theatrics almost came to a drastic end. She was preying on a target, a street pharmacist who was heavy in the streets named Paper Bag. Paper Bag's nose, like the others' noses, was wide open, but he had a keen way of analyzing his surroundings that Tina never could fathom. Paper Bag was ready to make her his exclusive woman, but first he had to make sure she would not do any flagrantly foul shit. Paper Bag had no problem spreading his wealth, buying her anything and everything she desired. But grungy bitches were a no-go.

Paper Bag decided to set a trap to see if Tina would go for the bait. He would leave a stack of counted currency lying around on occasion, then act like it had slipped his mind, just to make sure she wouldn't do him dirty. In Tina's mind, she assumed that he wouldn't even miss a thing if she were to help herself. Little did she know. She failed the test.

Paper Bag confronted Tina, who denied everything. But she seemed nervous—and a bit puzzled that he had noticed the missing money. Tina assumed she could suck him into an amnesia coma, then maybe he would forget the whole ordeal. Paper Bag gave in to her advances and then fell asleep as usual.

Tina figured she was in the clear since Paper Bag never again brought the missing money to her attention. Assuming everything was cool, she prepared to hit the gym one lonely afternoon. That afternoon, like she always did, she sprinted the six blocks to her destination with her earphones on full blast. She never heard the rowdy pack of females approaching. Sensing a shadow behind her, she looked back with one earphone out of her ear. That's when the group of wild hyenas beat her like Jesus in *The Passion of the Christ*. Tina suffered a major orange-juice-style beatdown, being beaten to a pulp. It would have been worse if it hadn't been for Polluten and Bigbits driving past. Deciding to intervene, the officers jumped out of their car. One of them screamed, "OK, that's enough!" The girls got the fuck outta dodge. Tina was spared. No arrest was made, but an informant was born.

Tina put the officers on the trail of Nitro, who was antisocial when it came to street business, she told them. She managed to give them his license plate number and the address of the place where she had let him redecorate her walls. The officers advised her to stay close and keep her eyes and ears open—do what she was good at so they could get what they needed. Tina now had a black hole in her soul because of Paper Bag's way of examining his surroundings. She took her orders to the cold place her heart used to be, cold as a pole in the winter.

Chapter 18

In the Meantime, it's get Swole and get Clean Time

Commonwealth state damn near got me nailed to the cross.
I knew I was doomed when the examination got crossed.
Going home wasn't my reality. Of course.
Fuck it. A clearer fate.
Fuck around and escape.
Prides a motherfucker.
Damn, should've pumped the brakes.

—Leery

Daydreaming, thumbing through the latest issue of *Blues & Rhythm*, Black lay back on his cot. While the quiet storm serenaded his ears, he started wishing life was a movie so he could rewind the tape. Reality had finally sunk in. Black tried to make the best of a bad situation. Even though he was strong, the bullshit was penetrative.

Mail was like a connection to home. A visit was like blowing air in his lungs. A simple weekend could turn into a lifetime of grief. The announcement that he had a visitor—who turned out to be an unusual visitor—damn near brought tears to his eyes.

He was taken to the visiting room. There was doubt written on his visitor's face. He could see she didn't trust him. He looked into the distance. She was an older, female version of him with the same facial features, but without the beard and hairdo. He sat down across from her. There was a moment of silence before he broke the ice.

"I was going to write to you," Black stated.

"You should have never been there in the first place. The problem is you still don't think you did anything to hurt me. You will always be free to do what you want, but you are not free from the consequences of your choice. The truth is, everybody is going to hurt you. You have to find the ones worth suffering for." Black's mom's words touched his soul. Pale-faced, he listened with a stream of tears rolling down his cheeks. A shiver raced down his spine, and a lump came to his throat. Black could literally feel the words that the first woman he'd loved—and the only woman he had ever loved—spoke with wisdom. With his faith restored, he realized he would do the time and not let the time do him.

Chapter 19

Get the Fuck outta Dodge

Shorty was like, "What you need? I got you."
I'm like, "Who you need to bleed? I pop Duke; I stop Duke.
He a memory." History fucking with a felony.
I'm just frontin' like Pharrell, dodging jail. Broken scale.
I can't measure it out. Assume I was ass out.
Started creeping in my enemy's house.

—Leery

Nitro had lain low since the strip had become hot like fish grease. Most of his little block huggers had gone through bullpen therapy. That let him know it was time for him to get the fuck outta dodge. Nitro was too big a player in the game to stand on the block and pitch the remaining work he had left. He decided to count his losses. The urge for some Chinese spareribs embraced him like a bitch after a stroke game. He hopped into his whip just to make his craving a reality. A block from his home, he was surrounded by cop cars and was ordered to step out of his vehicle.

"Step out of the car with your hands up," Officer Polluten said.

With the blicker on deck, Nitro had two choices: go out in a blaze, or stay cool as the Fonz. He put the pedal to the metal and peeled out. Thirty blocks and eighteen minutes later, he was in custody just like the others.

Nitro was now slouched in a chair. Behind the desk, listening to the possible things he could do to ensure his freedom, Polluten and Bigbits brought out some photos of a baby gangster whom Nitro frequently rolled with, along with photos of some other people.

"Are you familiar with the people in these pictures?"

"What happened to them?"

Nitro, all too familiar with the theatrics, just played naive. The officers threw all types of hypotheses his way. Nitro didn't even ask for a drink. Given the car chase and the blicker he'd been holding, he knew he was jammed up. But it wasn't anything serious. A master at poker would have been able to read the bluff. He knew the police were fishing. Even Stevie Wonder could have seen it.

I know what will get his attention, Officer Bigbits thought.

"Are you familiar with this young lady Tina?" Bigbits asked. The mention of Tina sparked a memory. Not dumb enough to mix pleasure and business, Nitro became skeptical about where this line of questioning was going. Two options came to mind: Tina had turned out to be a slut for the authorities, or she had team-lined their asses up. Nitro's thought was always that the less his female companion knew, the better, and he'd made sure she knew only a little. As for the loose ends still in the picture, he felt he was in pretty good shape.

"I know I'm going down for the blicker," Nitro replied to the officer. "But you are not going to put those bodies on me. Real shit, no perjury."

Chapter 20

A clearer Fate

> I Have Fought the Good Fight, I Have Finished the Race, I Have Kept the Faith

You can love me or hate me,
Play like my man and snake me.
trust no man but God cause.
Thats the one who made me.
Contemplating lately who praying
For my downfall. Middle finger to all y'all.
I take that back. I'm supposed to love y'all.
Wait. I'm a work in progress. I
Probably slug y'all with uplifting scriptures
To paint a perfect picture.
I been kissed by God. Lights out.
In the hallway. The devil missed his mark.
Whatever happen was meant to?
Happen through the grace with faith.
No matter what I was lacking, tell him your plan. He'll probably
Start laughing. How many non-believers? I'm just asking, even though
I'm four hundred plus six a gee. It still a need to just believe.

—Leery

Four years, eight months, and twenty-four days later, Tracey glided across the stage to accept her PhD diploma from the prestigious Arkansas State University. She was this year's valedictorian. All her loved ones were in attendance.

There to share her moment was her mother, Yaritza; her father, P.P.; and her baby boy, P.P. Jr., Porkin Bean Jeremy Jr., along with her newfound love, Jesus. She was as big as a house, eight months pregnant with her second child. Tears of joy escaped from her eyelids. She stood behind the podium and spoke to the crowd with her loved ones on her mind.

"Endeavors build mystique. Everybody knows the old saying 'What doesn't kill you only makes you stronger.' Well, there was a time when I wished I was dead so it would all be over. Or maybe just the people and the circumstances would just vanish into the air and be gone for eternity. I'm aware things happen for a reason. If God himself came to me personally and said, 'You're gonna go through this and that just to get to this,' I would've said, 'Miss me with that bullshit,' meaning the treachery, the lifestyle, the preference, the nurturing, the comeuppance, and the amorousness, so I may have a clearer fate.

Malicious Wound
(A Clearer Fate II)

Chapter 1

Ask God Why I'm Broke

> Broke no weed to smoke damn I hope I don't get
> bag sling dope,
> but I know the rope shine like egg yoke
> They say I'm nuts, like cashews,
> For lusting after stacks. What the broke lack,
> Strong arm and pitching, can
> Be justified, for that is just the facts.
>
> —Leery

She'd imagined this moment many times, but she never expected it to tear apart a strong bond. She had contemplated that true love was only an illusion. Crying became a daily ritual for Tracey. Lying at night next to her sleeping husband, Artie, she found that his snoring had become customary too. She dreaded the days of being alone, blaming herself for not being able to keep her husband home. He was aware of the lifestyle but assumed that he was a visionary, thinking that meaningless sex was suitable for a season. Still, Tracey realized that he was not ready to settle down and make her his priority. His previously occasional drug use had become constant. The brown water became an escape, and the industry groupies became his happy place. That alone put a damper on her sex life. Mr. Trick-and-Treat damn near blew through their savings in their joint bank account. But she was still glued to her husband, afraid to be alone, soaking her pillow with tears every time she thought about how things had turned out. Fresh out of school, she was unable to find work in her field, which left her with few choices to make ends meet.

With her old life behind her and two small mouths to feed, Tracey needed to have some additional income coming in to escape her past and set an example for her children. She was able to obtain a waitressing position at a neighborhood diner. Making six hundred fifty dollars a week plus tips was not her idea of living the good life with a college degree. On a usual Saturday for Tracey, for the umpteenth time, her tips and her paychecks were neck and neck. The first and second time, Tracey thought it was totally coincidental. After a month straight of the same pattern, she realized it had been orchestrated. She wasn't mad but was a little shocked. Suddenly her life didn't seem so useless.